DESTINY'S KALEIDOSCOPE

Unravelling the Colours of Fate

Vikas Parihar

Contents

Like the lotus rises gracefully
from muddy waters, so too does
destiny unfold its petals,
revealing the beauty
of a life's journey.

— Vikas Parihar

Prologue

In the vibrant heart of Mumbai, a city that pulsed with the frenetic energy of life and exuded an enigmatic allure all its own, there lived a man named Arjun. In the labyrinthine sprawl of crowded streets and towering structures, he was but a silhouette, a figure largely unnoticed in the kaleidoscope of faces that painted the daily tapestry of urban existence. Yet, beneath the surface of this seemingly ordinary life, a profound yearning simmered—a yearning that hinted at a desire to transcend the confines of routine and delve into the extraordinary.

At the age of 41, Arjun's days unfolded like a well-rehearsed play, each scene meticulously scripted within the parameters of societal expectations. His professional life, as an architect sculpting skyscrapers that mirrored his own unspoken dreams, played out against the backdrop of Mumbai's bustling metropolis. Each project carried not only the weight of concrete and steel but also the echoes of his aspirations and the silent yearning for a life less ordinary.

The city, a pulsating organism in its own right, whispered stories to Arjun as he navigated its chaotic streets. It was a narrative woven into the very fabric of the buildings he designed, the people he encountered, and the rhythm of life that echoed through the alleys and boulevards. His existence became a delicate dance, an intricate choreography that unfolded with every footstep—a dance that hinted at a restlessness beneath the surface.

Nights in Mumbai held a special magic, a time when the city's relentless energy took a momentary pause. It was during these quiet hours that Arjun felt the whispers of destiny, like elusive sirens beckoning him toward the extraordinary. In the hushed darkness, his mind wandered through the possibilities hidden within the ordinary, and the city itself seemed to hold its breath, waiting for the next chapter in his story to unfold.

The routine that bound Arjun also masked the complexities of his character. Behind the façade of a man caught in the humdrum of everyday life, there was a depth waiting to be explored—an inner world of dreams, conflicts, and unspoken desires. As he moved through the motions of his existence, a yearning for more, a hunger for experiences beyond the mundane, gnawed at the edges of his consciousness.

And so, when an unexpected twist of fate disrupted the predictable cadence of his life, Arjun found himself at a crossroads—a juncture where the choices made and chances taken would not only test his resilience and challenge his convictions but also unravel the intricacies of his own character. The symphony of destiny, once a distant melody, now crescendoed around him, inviting him to step beyond the boundaries of the ordinary into the vast expanse of the extraordinary.

In the serendipitous embrace of fate, a transformative spark ignited within the heart of Arjun. It happened in the lively expanse of a bustling café, where his gaze collided with a pair of eyes that seemed to harbor the universe's deepest secrets. Aaradhya, a woman adorned with enigmatic allure and an insatiable curiosity, entered his life with the force of a whirlwind. Their worlds converged like celestial bodies in a cosmic collision, and at that moment, the symphony of their lives commenced, playing in harmonious unison.

The crossroads of destiny had swung open a door to a realm Arjun had never dared to fathom. As he delved deeper into the labyrinth of his own soul, Aaradhya emerged as his guide, a confidante in this intricate dance with destiny. Their connection deepened through conversations that stretched into the early hours of the morning and late-night strolls along the shores of Mumbai's coastline. Together, they embarked on a profound journey that would challenge their beliefs, reshape their aspirations, and unveil the kaleidoscopic wonder hidden within the seemingly mundane.

As companions, they unraveled the threads of resilience that had woven the fabric of their lives. Adversity became the catalyst for Arjun's strengths to blossom, and his weaknesses transformed into stepping stones toward personal growth. The city of Mumbai, with its labyrinthine streets and concealed alleys, served as a canvas for their exploration—a dynamic backdrop against which their journey unfolded.

Amidst laughter and tears, joy and heartache, they uncovered the power of embracing the unknown. They danced through the cadence of strength, navigated the echoes of euphoria, and found harmony in the synchronicities woven into the fabric of their path. As their bond deepened, so did their comprehension of the symphony connecting all living beings—a melody of existence transcending the boundaries of time and space. In the shared chapters of their lives, Arjun and Aaradhya discovered a profound truth: that within the tapestry of the ordinary lies an extraordinary richness waiting to be unveiled.

As Arjun's metamorphosis unfolded, he discovered that destiny's tapestry was not a static, unchanging design etched in stone, but a living, breathing entity that responded to the choices he made. Each encounter, every decision, became a brushstroke on the canvas of his fate. The symphony of resilience that had accompanied him on this transformative journey echoed the rhythm of life itself—full of unexpected crescendos and tranquil interludes.

Over the three years since that fateful meeting, Arjun and Aaradhya had embarked on a profound exploration of their own souls. Their journey took them to the farthest corners of India, from the majestic Himalayas to the serene backwaters of Kerala. Each place they visited, every person they encountered, added a new layer to their understanding of resilience, a new note to their symphony.

Their experiences had reshaped their perceptions of success and fulfillment. Liberated from the confines of conventional measures of achievement, Arjun realized that the true essence of life lay not solely in reaching a destination but in savoring the journey itself. His once-muted dreams found a voice, harmonizing with the rhythm of his newfound purpose.

The symphony of resilience that Arjun had conducted in his own life resonated with those who crossed his path. His story, a testament to the human spirit's capacity to adapt, evolve, and triumph, touched the hearts of millions who followed his journey. Letters poured in from far and wide, each one a testament to the symphony that Arjun had unwittingly composed.

Standing on the same rooftop where their journey had begun, overlooking the sprawling city of Mumbai, Arjun and Aaradhya reflected on the kaleidoscope of their experiences—a mosaic of memories illustrating their evolution. They understood that life's tapestry was shaped not only by destiny's hand but also by the choices they had made, the resilience they had nurtured, and the melodies they had composed.

Their story, a symphony of resilience, wielded the power to transform lives. It served as a reminder that within the chaos of life's dance, an underlying harmony waited to be discovered. As the sun dipped below the horizon, casting a golden hue across the city, Arjun and

Aaradhya stood hand in hand, ready to continue their exploration of life's infinite possibilities.

The symphony of resilience had become their legacy, a melody that would resonate through the hearts of those who dared to dream. With a shared sense of purpose and a commitment to embracing life's kaleidoscopic beauty, they stepped into the next chapter of their journey, eager to compose new melodies, encounter new challenges, and uncover new shades of resilience. And as the city lights flickered to life around them, they walked forward, their symphony echoing through the ages.

— Vikas

Unveiling Destiny's Tapestry

In the intricate web of existence, where lives entwine like threads in a vast tapestry, pivotal moments await, poised to redefine destinies. This is the chronicle of an extraordinary journey undertaken by Arjun, a 41-year-old Indian man, navigating the transformative odyssey through the bustling labyrinth of urban life.

Enter Arjun, an unassuming figure leading what appears to be an ordinary life in the vibrant city of Mumbai. Ensnared in the monotonous routines of daily existence, he hungers for a deeper purpose, a profound significance to lend meaning to his being. Unbeknownst to him, a seemingly trivial invitation to a local gathering is about to unravel the intricate design of his fate.

With salt-and-pepper hair and eyes reflecting the wisdom of a life well-lived, Arjun stands as a man who has weathered life's storms but remains on the cusp of discovering the true essence of his journey. As he navigates the labyrinthine alleys of Mumbai, he assumes the role of a silent observer, attuned to the ceaseless rhythm of the city—the persistent hum of car horns, the hurried cadence of footsteps, and the symphony of life unfolding at every street corner.

One evening, amid the cacophony of the city, a hand-written invitation slips under Arjun's door. It beckons him to a quaint gathering hosted by a neighbor—an artist renowned for paintings that breathe life into still canvases. Despite his initial hesitations, Arjun decides to attend, drawn by the enigmatic aura that envelops the artist and the promise of uncovering layers of meaning beneath the surface of his own existence.

As Arjun steps into the artist's studio, the walls adorned with vivid strokes of color immediately seize his attention. Each painting, a narrative in itself, weaves tales untold. The artist, clad in flamboyant attire and enveloped in an aura of profound calm, exudes an air of mystery. Intrigued, Arjun senses that beneath the paint-stained hands lies a reservoir of knowledge waiting to be unearthed.

"Welcome," the artist warmly interrupts Arjun's thoughts. "I'm glad you could make it."

Arjun nods, reciprocating with a tentative smile. "Thank you for having me. Your paintings are truly remarkable."

The gathering unfolds into an evening of captivating conversations, where each person shares fragments of their lives, akin to pieces of a puzzle awaiting assembly. Amid the guests, Arjun encounters a wise elder whose eyes crinkle with laughter as he imparts age-old wisdom with a modern twist. There's also the free-spirited traveler, weaving tales of wanderlust and adventure that kindle a yearning within Arjun's heart.

As the night deepens, Arjun becomes engrossed in stories that resonate with the deepest recesses of his soul. The artist, the elder, and the traveler—each seemingly possessing a key to unlock life's mysteries. Their wisdom, combined with Arjun's own introspection, sets in motion a series of events that will unravel the tapestry of existence, exposing the interconnectedness of every thread.

Through the artist's vivid strokes, Arjun learns the art of finding beauty in the mundane, of drawing inspiration from the most unexpected places. The elder's timeless wisdom opens Arjun's eyes to the cyclical nature of life— the ebb and flow of joy and sorrow, success and failure. The traveler's boundless curiosity ignites a spark within Arjun, compelling him to step out of his comfort zone and embrace the unknown.

In the ensuing days, Arjun's life undergoes a profound metamorphosis. He finds himself irresistibly drawn to new experiences and unexpected encounters that challenge the preconceived notions he once held. Forgotten dreams are revisited, and passions long dormant are rekindled. With each deliberate step, Arjun begins to discern a purpose—a calling that transcends the confines of his own existence.

Amidst the vibrant chaos of Mumbai, Arjun uncovers a revelation: every individual he encounters has a unique story to tell, a thread contributing to the rich tapestry of life. From the chaiwala on the street corner to the elderly couple in the park, each person adds their distinct notes to the symphony of existence. The city itself becomes a metaphor for life, where the bustling streets mirror the ceaseless journey of the human spirit.

As Arjun delves deeper into life's intricacies, he realizes that destiny's tapestry is far from a static creation. It is a dynamic work in progress, shaped by choices, connections, and the courage to embrace uncertainty. The threads of fate transcend the boundaries of time, place, and background, uniting every living being in a cosmic dance of interconnectedness.

Through moments of laughter and tears, triumphs and tribulations, Arjun discovers that life's meaning is not derived from a single defining moment but from the continuous evolution of one's being. The extraordinary, he learns, lies hidden within the ordinary, awaiting discovery by those brave enough to embark on the journey of self-discovery.

Join Arjun as he weaves his legacy, a tapestry that transcends the boundaries of his own life, becoming a source of inspiration for generations to come. "Unveiling Destiny's Tapestry" is more than just a story; it is an invitation to explore the tapestry of your own existence, to recognize the beauty in the mundane, and embrace the interconnectedness of all life. Through Arjun's journey, may you discover echoes of your own destiny woven into the fabric of the universe's grand design.

The Ordinary Becomes Extraordinary

April 1, 2021

A Glimpse of Destiny

In the pulsating heart of Mumbai, where dreams collided headlong with the stark reality of existence, Arjun Kapoor dwelled—a man straddling the line between ordinary and extraordinary. His passion for marketing, an inferno that blazed within him, traced its origins back to the captivating world of storytelling. For Arjun, marketing was more than a career; it was the art of weaving emotions, shaping perceptions, and etching indelible memories on the tapestry of life.

From a young age, Arjun found himself captivated by the hypnotic allure of advertisements that danced across his television screen. The mundane transformed into the extraordinary before his eyes, and the spellbinding artistry of marketing became a siren song that beckoned him. Yet, Arjun's journey into this realm was clouded by the uncertainty of his middle-class upbringing, where stability and financial security were worshipped as the holy grails of success.

In the face of familial expectations nudging him toward the safer shores of conventional professions like engineering or medicine, Arjun's inner fire refused to be extinguished. With audacious courage, he chose to traverse the unpredictable landscape of marketing, a journey that would redefine not only his career but his entire existence.

His initiation into the professional world took place at a modest advertising agency. Fresh out of academia, Arjun sought to unleash his creativity upon the world. Little did he know that the corridors of marketing were a battleground where unyielding deadlines, demanding clients, and cutthroat competition awaited him.

Undeterred, Arjun pressed on. Each day, he poured his heart into his work, striving to prove himself in a realm where success seemed elusive. But as time flowed and seasons changed, doubt crept in. Was he destined for a life that mirrored the ordinary, just another face in the crowd?

One fateful evening, weary after a day that had demanded every ounce of his being, Arjun opted for an uncharted path home. Destiny, in its subtle machinations, led him to a quaint bookstore nestled among the towering structures of the city—a haven of boundless possibilities.

The bookstore's shelves were a treasure trove of knowledge, with books of myriad genres whispering promises of new beginnings. In this literary sanctuary, Arjun's eyes fell upon a book adorned with a lotus on its cover—a symbol of resilience and enlightenment.

Intrigued, he seized the book, revealing its title: "The Book of Infinite Possibilities: Embracing the Magic of Life," penned by the elusive "Sage of Serendipity." Page after page, Arjun was drawn into its profound wisdom. The book spoke of embracing life's uncertainties, discovering beauty in the unexpected, and the enchanting power of synchronicity.

Arjun found himself spellbound. Each word felt like a coded message meant exclusively for him, reigniting the embers of his passion. The concept of serendipity, the idea that life's twists and turns could lead him to his true calling, resonated deeply.

With the book as his guide, Arjun embarked on a transformative journey. Days melted into weeks as he immersed himself in its teachings. "The Book of Infinite Possibilities" was a revelation, unlocking doors to a realm beyond conventional marketing. It revealed that marketing was not just about selling products; it was a conduit for forging connections, understanding aspirations, and touching lives.

Fueled by the book's teachings, Arjun viewed his work through a new lens. No longer a mere ladder to corporate success, it became a canvas for impacting the world. He infused his campaigns with the magic he had discovered, creating stories that resonated with millions.

One remarkable campaign centered on organic skincare products marked a paradigm shift. Eschewing celebrity endorsements, Arjun turned his spotlight on the farmers behind the natural ingredients. Venturing into remote villages, he captured their lives and passions, empowering them and catalyzing change within their communities.

As word of Arjun's innovative approach spread, a global marketing agency took notice. Impressed by his creativity and commitment to making a difference, they extended an offer—an opportunity to work on international campaigns and collaborate with industry luminaries.

However, with global opportunities came fresh challenges. Arjun grappled with self-doubt anew, questioning his ability to meet the heightened expectations of global campaigns.

"You've got this, Arjun," his friend Rahul reassured over coffee, offering a smile that carried the weight of shared triumphs. "Remember, you've turned challenges into stepping stones before."

Empowered by the whispers of destiny, Arjun redefined creativity. His campaigns became bridges that connected cultures, touching shared human experiences. Accolades poured in from clients and peers, yet Arjun remained grounded, always acknowledging the role of serendipity in his journey.

Then, an email arrived—an invitation to speak at a Barcelona marketing conference. An opportunity to share his insights and experiences on a global stage. **"Barcelona!" Arjun exclaimed, reading the email aloud. "Looks like destiny's inviting me on a global tour."**

Standing before a diverse audience in Barcelona, Arjun felt a profound sense of gratitude. The bookstore, the book, the journey—they had all conspired to lead him here. In his speech, he wove tales of perseverance, resilience, and serendipity. His words resonated, forging connections that spanned continents.

After his speech, lines formed with eager faces sharing serendipitous tales. A new chapter unfolded—Arjun's role as a catalyst for change. His campaigns acquired a deeper purpose, empowering the marginalized, championing social causes, and advocating for environmental sustainability.

As the pages of Arjun's story turned, the lotus that once adorned a book cover now symbolized not only resilience and enlightenment but the intricate dance of fate and choice that had guided him through a journey of self-discovery—a journey that transcended marketing and left an indelible mark on the lives he touched.

Embracing the Magic

Arjun's ascent to fame as a marketing virtuoso surged, drawing an increasing demand for his insights. The alchemy of his creativity and serendipity stirred the minds of marketers and entrepreneurs. Invitations poured in for him to headline conferences, where his enthralling narratives and experiences held audiences spellbound. He seamlessly interwove campaign strategies with moments of vulnerability, compelling listeners to transcend the confines of conventional marketing.

Within the whirlwind of Arjun's rising prominence, his calendar transformed into a mosaic of cities. From the bustling streets of New York City to the serene enclaves of Kyoto, he absorbed fresh perspectives, enriching his comprehension of the ever-shifting marketing landscape.

Amidst the transient nature of flights and hotel stays, Arjun diligently recorded thoughts inspired by "The Book of Infinite Possibilities." These reflections coalesced into a magnum opus: "The Serendipity Code: Unleashing Your Marketing Genius." With each meticulously chosen word, he pushed past the boundaries of traditional marketing, advocating for the enchantment of life as a formidable force in achieving success.

Chapter titles bore time stamps, enhancing reader immersion. Arjun's narrative unfolded seamlessly, with temporal markers guiding readers through a vivid journey. These subtle cues anchored the tale, inviting readers to traverse alongside him.

Descriptive prose painted scenes and events with vivid strokes. From the frenetic streets of Mumbai to the tranquil heights of Himachal Pradesh, Arjun's words transported readers, evoking a tapestry of senses and emotions.

"You know," mused Arjun during a panel discussion in Tokyo, "the essence of marketing lies in embracing the unexpected. It's akin to discovering a concealed treasure amidst the chaos of life."

Beyond mere settings, Arjun's characters underwent profound evolution, laying bare their thoughts, emotions, and motivations. Inner conflicts unfolded, and readers found themselves empathizing, sharing an emotional odyssey.

Arjun adeptly portrayed emotions through action, amplifying pivotal moments. Doubt and fear quickened pulses; clarity and triumph kindled inspiration, resonating with readers' own struggles.

The pacing orchestrated an immersive experience. Action harmonized with contemplation, enabling readers to savor Arjun's insights.

Themes of destiny, resilience, and self-discovery seamlessly interwove. Each chapter wove these themes into Arjun's narrative, with the lotus symbolizing resilience, adding a layer of depth.

"Sometimes, the most extraordinary campaigns stem from ordinary stories," Arjun remarked to a fellow marketer in Paris. "It's in the mundane that we uncover the extraordinary."

Arjun's unwavering voice and distinctive style ensured the symphony of storytelling flowed. A seamless rhythm resonated, forging a profound connection.

Carefully interwoven flashbacks added context without disruption. As the book approached its zenith, Arjun skillfully tied loose ends, providing readers with closure and a sense of transformation.

"Life isn't a singular note; it's a symphony," Arjun declared during a workshop in London. "Serendipity introduces the unexpected harmonies that make it beautiful."

The closing chapters left readers invigorated. Arjun's journey echoed, underscoring life's masterpiece woven by destiny and serendipity.

Empowered by "The Book of Infinite Possibilities" and the enchantment of serendipity, Arjun confronted an infinite future. Aligned with his purpose, he knew serendipity would continue to be his guiding light.

Arjun grasped that this moment marked not just an ending but the genesis of something new. Uncharted chapters lay ahead, with the enchantment of serendipity promising boundless possibilities.

With a heart brimming with gratitude, Arjun embraced what lay before him. Life, he understood, meant daring to dream beyond the visible, recognizing that serendipity's code was orchestrating a life devoted to creativity, compassion, and limitless opportunity.

In every encounter, Arjun discovered the gentle touch of serendipity—a reminder that life's intricacies were integral to a grand design. A conversation with a street artist in Rome ignited a campaign celebrating hidden talents, while a chance encounter with an old friend led to a collaboration that transcended boundaries.

"It's not merely about selling products," Arjun emphasized during a seminar in Sydney. "It's about crafting connections, about nurturing stories that resonate with the core of the human experience."

Arjun's journey resonated far beyond the realm of marketing. As his story spread, individuals from diverse walks of life found solace in his philosophy. From the vibrant streets of Mumbai to the towering skyscrapers of New York, people shared how they, too, had been touched by the grace of serendipity.

Amidst the acclaim and accomplishments, Arjun's purpose remained unwavering. He recognized himself not merely as a marketer but as a storyteller, a messenger of serendipity's magic. In every speech, every campaign, he wove the threads of destiny, creating a tapestry of inspiration.

"Serendipity isn't a chance event; it's a dance with the universe," Arjun shared during a TED Talk in Vancouver. "And when we step onto the dance floor with an open heart, life's music guides us to extraordinary places."

As the inaugural chapter of his extraordinary journey drew to a close, Arjun felt a profound sense of gratitude. The serendipitous encounters, the unexpected lessons— they had all led him to this moment—a moment where he stood on the threshold of infinite possibilities.

With each heartbeat, Arjun embraced the rhythm of serendipity. He knew that destiny's tapestry was vast and intricate, a masterpiece that unfolded with every step he took. Venturing into the unwritten chapters, he carried with him the wisdom that serendipity was not just a stroke of luck; it was a symphony of the soul, a melody guiding him toward the extraordinary in the ordinary.

And so, with the magic of serendipity as his guide, Arjun stepped into tomorrow, prepared to continue his journey of unveiling the tapestry of existence—one thread, one moment, one serendipitous encounter at a time.

“

Turn challenges into creative
opportunities, and everyday
life transforms into something
extraordinary

”

2

Serendipitous Encounters

June 16, 2021

A Chance Meeting

Arjun's reputation as a transformative marketing leader soared, taking him around the globe, from captivating keynote speeches to high-profile industry events. His innovative vision set the stage for a turning point, and it all began with a flight to a prestigious marketing conference in New York City.

Entering the conference venue, Arjun felt the palpable excitement. The hall buzzed with marketing professionals eager to glean insights from industry luminaries. Confidence radiated from Arjun as he took the stage, weaving a tapestry of wisdom that held the audience spellbound. Thunderous applause echoed, affirming the impact of his eloquence.

Post-keynote, a line formed with attendees, among them Riya, a young marketing strategist with admiration gleaming in her eyes. Meeting Arjun was a dream for Riya, an aspiring marketer who recently launched her consultancy firm.

Arjun, with his warm demeanor, greeted Riya. "Thank you, Riya. Meeting young talents like you who are passionate about marketing is heartening. What brings you to the conference?"

Determined, Riya shared her aspirations and eagerness to learn. Arjun admired her ambition, sensing in her the same hunger for knowledge that fueled him in his younger days. Their meeting felt destined.

As the conference concluded, Arjun and Riya exchanged contact information, promising to stay connected. Over the weeks, email conversations evolved into video calls. Arjun witnessed Riya's growth and saw in her the potential he once recognized in himself.

Their mentorship deepened into a unique bond—a friendship transcending age and experience. They discussed not just marketing but life, philosophy, and the greater purpose of their work. Arjun emphasized using marketing for positive change, shaping culture, and inspiring progress.

"Riya," Arjun said passionately, "we have the power to influence minds and inspire action through marketing. Let's use this power responsibly and make a difference in the world."

Riya nodded, feeling a deep connection. Their mentorship shaped her not just as a marketer but as a person. Arjun's guidance gave her the confidence to take risks, challenge conventions, and think outside the box.

Their bond strengthened, and Arjun saw himself as both a mentor and friend to Riya. He joyfully watched her career flourish as she fearlessly pursued innovative campaigns. Riya's consultancy gained recognition, and accolades followed her impactful campaigns.

A groundbreaking campaign for a social development organization showcased Riya's potential. Arjun praised, "You've not only created an impactful campaign but also touched the lives of so many people. This is the power of using marketing for a purpose."

Riya beamed with gratitude, knowing Arjun's mentorship played a pivotal role. Their shared mission emerged—to use marketing as a force for positive change. Together, they embarked on creating campaigns that sold products and touched hearts, changing lives.

Their shared vision led to an extraordinary collaboration challenging the essence of marketing, leaving an indelible mark on the industry. Arjun left Riya with a final piece of advice, "It's not just about being extraordinary in what you do; it's about inspiring others to find their own extraordinary within. That's the true essence of leadership."

With renewed determination, Riya embraced the next phase of her journey, knowing she had a mentor, a friend, and a partner in Arjun. Little did they know their serendipitous encounter was just the beginning of an incredible adventure.

Their mentorship flourished, leading to new adventures. They became a sought-after duo, delivering joint presentations that left audiences inspired. Beyond the stage, they initiated workshops and mentorship programs, paying forward the knowledge they had received.

Their impact extended beyond marketing. The "Empower HER" movement aimed to empower women entrepreneurs globally, sparking a movement for female empowerment. Arjun and Riya's campaigns became cultural phenomena, inspiring change on a global scale.

Their work redefined marketing's purpose, shaping perceptions, driving conversations, and leaving a positive mark on the world. Through their joint efforts, Arjun and Riya transformed not just the marketing landscape but also their own lives.

As the years passed, their collaboration continued to make waves. Arjun realized his journey mirrored the transformative guidance he had received from "The Book of Infinite Possibilities." It was a cycle of learning, growth, and empowerment—an everlasting legacy of wisdom passed to the next generation.

Arjun's feelings for Riya evolved. He found himself thinking about her even outside their professional exchanges. He admired her passion, determination, and her view of marketing as a canvas for creativity and positive change.

One night, Arjun decided to be honest about his feelings. In an email to Riya, he expressed, "Riya, our mentorship has meant more to me than I can express. I value our connection deeply, and I can't help but wonder if there's something more between us."

As the email winged its way to Riya's inbox, Arjun couldn't help but smile. The ordinary had truly become extraordinary, and the tapestry of their connection wove a narrative of infinite possibilities.

Riya's response arrived, carrying a mix of emotions and anticipation. She appreciated Arjun's honesty and vulnerability, acknowledging the unique blend of mentorship and connection that had grown between them.

"Arjun, your mentorship has been a guiding light in my journey. I, too, have felt a connection that goes beyond the professional realm. Let's explore this, not just as mentors and mentees but as two souls navigating a shared path."

Their acknowledgment marked a shift in their relationship—a transition from mentorship to something more profound. As Arjun and Riya delved into the uncharted territories of their connection, they discovered a harmonious balance between professional collaboration and personal exploration.

Their shared ventures continued, and the dynamic duo became a beacon in the marketing world. Their joint presentations and workshops continued to inspire, fostering a community of aspiring marketers eager to learn from their collective wisdom.

One day, as Arjun and Riya prepared for a TED Talk, they reflected on the extraordinary journey that had brought them together. The stage became a canvas where their shared vision painted a picture of creativity, compassion, and the boundless power of serendipity.

"Riya," Arjun said backstage, "our story is a testament to the magic of serendipity. It's not just about the campaigns we create but the impact we have on each other and those we touch through our work."

The TED Talk became a pivotal moment, not just for Arjun and Riya but for everyone who listened. Their narrative unfolded, seamlessly blending professional insights with personal revelations. The audience witnessed a genuine connection, a shared journey that transcended the confines of the stage.

As their TED Talk concluded with a standing ovation, Arjun and Riya realized the magnitude of their influence. Their story became a symbol of possibility, a reminder that meaningful connections could emerge from the unexpected corners of life.

Beyond the accolades, Arjun and Riya continued to explore the depths of their connection. They embraced the ebb and flow of their relationship, recognizing that, like any masterpiece, it required nuance, care, and a willingness to evolve.

Their joint campaigns evolved into movements, leaving an indelible mark on societal conversations. The impact of their initiatives extended beyond marketing metrics—measuring not just sales but the positive change they inspired.

One day, as they stood on the rooftop of their shared office space, overlooking the city that had witnessed the evolution of their journey, Arjun spoke with a sense of fulfillment.

"Riya, our collaboration has surpassed even my wildest expectations. But it's not just about what we've achieved; it's about the legacy we're creating. The ripple effect of our work goes beyond us, shaping the future of marketing."

Riya nodded, her eyes reflecting a similar sense of accomplishment. "Arjun, our journey is a testament to the extraordinary power of serendipity. It's a reminder that, in the tapestry of life, every thread, every encounter, contributes to the masterpiece."

Their connection, now a tapestry woven with threads of mentorship, friendship, and a shared vision, continued to inspire. Arjun and Riya knew that their story was still unfolding, with chapters yet to be written.

As they looked toward the horizon, they embraced the uncertainty of the future. Destiny had intertwined their paths, and they walked forward with open hearts, ready to uncover the serendipitous surprises that awaited them.

The ordinary had indeed become extraordinary, and the magic of serendipity continued to guide Arjun and Riya on their journey of creativity, compassion, and the extraordinary possibilities that lay ahead.

The Unconventional Collaboration

Emboldened by the success of the first installation, Arjun and Riya took "The Canvas of Change" to different corners of the world. From the vibrant streets of Rio de Janeiro to the serene landscapes of Kyoto, each location brought forth a unique chapter in the campaign.

In Rio, the installation focused on environmental conservation. Giant sculptures crafted from recycled materials conveyed a powerful message about sustainability. Visitors engaged in workshops to create their eco-friendly art, fostering a sense of collective responsibility for the planet.

Kyoto witnessed an immersive experience celebrating cultural diversity. Traditional art forms intertwined with modern expressions, showcasing the richness of human heritage. The campaign not only celebrated the beauty of diversity but also emphasized the importance of inclusivity in a globalized world.

As "The Canvas of Change" unfolded, it became evident that the campaign was more than just a marketing endeavor. It had transformed into a movement that harnessed the universal language of art to address pressing global issues. Arjun and Riya's unconventional approach resonated with audiences far beyond the realms of traditional advertising.

Media outlets and influencers took notice, amplifying the campaign's impact. Soon, the hashtag #CanvasOfChange trended globally, creating a community of advocates who believed in the transformative power of art to drive positive change.

During a press conference in Paris, Arjun shared his thoughts on the campaign's success. "Art has the ability to transcend boundaries and touch the soul. 'The Canvas of Change' is not just about selling a product; it's about leveraging the emotional connection that art fosters to inspire meaningful action."

Riya added, "We wanted to redefine how people perceive marketing. It's not just about creating awareness; it's about creating a movement that leaves a lasting legacy. 'The Canvas of Change' is a testament to the idea that marketing can be a force for good in the world."

As the campaign gained momentum, Arjun and Riya were invited to speak at prestigious events and conferences. Their unconventional approach became a case study for marketers worldwide. They emphasized the need for authenticity, purpose, and emotional resonance in an era saturated with traditional advertising.

In the midst of their global journey, Arjun and Riya continued to mentor aspiring marketers. They conducted workshops, sharing the insights and lessons they had gleaned from "The Canvas of Change." Young talents embraced the idea that marketing could be a catalyst for positive impact, not just a means of selling products.

In a TED Talk in New York City, Arjun summarized the essence of their journey. "Marketing, at its core, is about connecting with people on a profound level. 'The Canvas of Change' taught us that when you infuse creativity, authenticity, and a purpose-driven narrative, marketing becomes a tool for societal transformation."

The success of the campaign had a ripple effect on the industry. Companies started reevaluating their marketing strategies, seeking ways to integrate purpose and social responsibility into their narratives. Arjun and Riya had inadvertently sparked a paradigm shift in the marketing landscape.

However, amidst the accolades and recognition, Arjun and Riya remained grounded. They knew that the true impact of their journey was measured not just in campaigns but in the lives touched and changed. The children in Mumbai, the environmental enthusiasts in Rio, and the diverse communities in Kyoto—all were a testament to the power of storytelling and art.

As "The Canvas of Change" continued its global tour, Arjun and Riya were already contemplating their next venture. Their journey had become a testament to the belief that marketing when guided by purpose and creativity, could be a force for positive transformation. The canvas of their extraordinary story remained open, ready to capture the infinite possibilities that serendipity continued to unveil.

"The Canvas of Change" had become a beacon of inspiration, attracting attention not only from the marketing community but also from city officials, cultural organizations, and philanthropic foundations. Cities around the world competed to host the next installation, eager to be a part of the transformative movement Arjun and Riya had sparked.

The duo carefully selected locations that aligned with the campaign's themes, ensuring each new installment addressed diverse societal challenges. From revitalizing urban spaces to advocating for mental health awareness, "The Canvas of Change" evolved into a dynamic platform for addressing pressing issues through the lens of art and storytelling.

The impact of the campaign extended beyond the installations themselves. Local communities embraced the messages, and grassroots movements emerged, inspired by the ethos of positive change. Arjun and Riya's collaboration had become a catalyst for collective action, illustrating the profound influence marketing could wield in shaping societal perspectives.

The campaign's success also attracted partnerships with influential artists, musicians, and creatives who were drawn to the authenticity and purpose embedded in "The Canvas of Change." Collaborations with renowned figures further amplified the campaign's reach, turning it into a global cultural phenomenon.

During an interview in London, Riya reflected on the journey. "What started as a conversation about redefining marketing has become a movement that transcends borders. 'The Canvas of Change' is a testament to the idea that when creativity and purpose converge, they can spark conversations that resonate on a global scale."

Arjun echoed her sentiments. "Our journey has shown us the incredible potential of storytelling and art in shaping societal narratives. It's a reminder that marketing, at its core, is about understanding human experiences and using that understanding to create positive change."

Amidst their globe-trotting adventures, Arjun and Riya remained connected to their roots, returning to Mumbai, where it all began. The city, with its vibrant energy, served as a constant source of inspiration for their work. The local communities, once the focus of their initial installation, now celebrated the global impact that had originated within their midst.

In a reflective moment during a rooftop event overlooking the Mumbai skyline, Arjun shared, "Our journey started with the belief that marketing could be more than just a transaction. Now, we witness the ripple effect of that belief, and it's a testament to the interconnectedness of stories and the power of collaboration."

Riya added, "Our mentorship has become a shared mission. We not only guide young marketers but also empower them to believe in the potential of their own narratives. 'The Canvas of Change' is a symbol of what happens when individuals come together with a shared vision for positive transformation."

As Arjun and Riya continued to navigate the dynamic landscape of marketing, their impact expanded beyond campaigns. They became advocates for ethical and purpose-driven marketing practices, urging industry leaders to consider the broader societal implications of their work.

The next chapter of their journey was marked by a commitment to sustainability and social responsibility. Collaborating with environmental organizations, "The Green Canvas" emerged as a sequel to their previous successes. This new venture aimed to raise awareness about environmental issues and inspire collective action for a sustainable future.

Arjun and Riya, now recognized as pioneers in the realm of purpose-driven marketing, remained humble amid their achievements. The lessons learned from "The Canvas of Change" had become guiding principles for marketers worldwide, influencing a shift towards campaigns that not only sold products but also contributed to the betterment of society.

Their legacy was not just a portfolio of successful campaigns but a testament to the transformative power of collaboration, creativity, and a shared vision for positive change. As they looked ahead to new horizons, Arjun and Riya knew that their journey had become a perpetual exploration of the infinite possibilities that awaited them and the world of marketing they sought to redefine.

In those moments, Arjun and Riya discovered a friendship that transcended the professional realm. They celebrated victories together and found solace in each other during challenges. The unspoken understanding between them fostered an environment where creativity flourished, ideas flowed seamlessly, and the lines between work and friendship blurred.

Their collaboration wasn't without its share of disagreements, yet these differences became opportunities for growth. Arjun's methodical approach sometimes clashed with Riya's instinctive flair, but instead of hindering progress, it enriched their creative process. They learned to appreciate the beauty in their diversity of thought, and it reflected in the richness of their campaigns.

As the duo continued to make waves in the marketing world, their influence reached beyond industry boundaries. Universities and business schools invited them to share their journey, turning the narrative of "The Canvas of Change" into a case study for aspiring marketers. Arjun and Riya embraced this role, recognizing the responsibility that came with being torchbearers of a new era in marketing.

During a guest lecture at a renowned business school, Arjun emphasized, "Innovation doesn't thrive in isolation. It's born from diverse perspectives colliding and coalescing. Riya and I may have different approaches, but it's the synergy between us that creates something truly remarkable."

Riya added, "The essence of our partnership lies not just in the campaigns we create but in the journey we share. It's about turning the ordinary into extraordinary, not just in marketing but in life itself."

Their story became a beacon for young professionals navigating the complexities of the corporate world. Messages flooded in from aspiring marketers inspired by the authenticity and impact of Arjun and Riya's journey. The duo responded with humility, recognizing that their success was not just personal but a testament to the potential within each person to create positive change.

"The Canvas of Change" continued to evolve, with new installations addressing global challenges, from environmental sustainability to mental health awareness. Arjun and Riya's commitment to purpose-driven marketing remained unwavering, a guiding principle that influenced not only their campaigns but also their interactions with the world.

As they stood together on the stage of a global marketing summit, Arjun spoke to the audience, "Our journey is a testament to the belief that marketing, at its core, is a force that can shape perceptions, challenge norms, and inspire action. The canvas of change is not just ours; it's a canvas we invite everyone to paint. Every story, every idea has the potential to be a stroke on that canvas, creating a masterpiece of positive transformation."

Riya echoed his sentiment, "We often underestimate the power we hold as marketers. Let's use it to create a world where purpose and profit coexist, where every campaign is a step towards a better tomorrow."

The applause that followed was not just for their words but for the authenticity and impact that Arjun and Riya had brought to the world of marketing. As they stepped off the stage, they knew that their journey was far from over. The canvas of change was still unfurling, and with every stroke, they continued to redefine the narrative of marketing—one of empathy, compassion, and the extraordinary power to make a difference.

As the canvas of their collaboration continued to unfold, Arjun and Riya navigated the delicate dance of their evolving connection. The unspoken emotions lingered between them, adding a layer of complexity to their partnership. The success of their campaigns had woven their professional lives together, and the lines between mentorship and something deeper became increasingly blurred.

One evening, after a particularly challenging presentation, Arjun and Riya found themselves on a quiet street, away from the bustling city. The moon hung low, casting a soft glow around them. Breaking the silence, Riya's voice was gentle, "Arjun, do you ever wonder where this journey is leading us?"

Arjun paused, feeling the weight of her question. "I do, Riya. But I also believe that sometimes, the journey is more important than the destination."

Her gaze held his, reflecting the moonlight in her eyes. "I've learned so much from you, Arjun. You've not just been a mentor but a guiding light in my life."

He smiled, his voice tender. "And you've brought a new energy to my world, Riya. Your passion, your perspective—it's been a breath of fresh air."

In that moonlit moment, the unspoken emotions surrounded them like the night air—fragile and uncertain, yet undeniably present. They understood that their journey was far from over, and the chapters yet to be written held the promise of discovery and transformation.

As the weeks passed, the dynamics of their relationship continued to shift. Late nights at the office turned into lingering glances and shared laughter carried a resonance that echoed beyond the boardroom. The unspoken tension between them added depth to their collaboration, a layer of complexity that fueled both their creativity and internal conflicts.

One day, during a quiet moment in the office, Riya broke the silence, her words carefully chosen. "Arjun, our journey has been extraordinary, and I value our connection more than words can express."

He met her gaze, a mixture of vulnerability and sincerity in her eyes. "Riya, our collaboration has been the highlight of my career. You've brought a vibrancy to our work that's irreplaceable."

As they acknowledged the unspoken undercurrents of their relationship, a shared understanding emerged— that their connection was more than a professional alliance. Yet, the intricacies of personal feelings remained delicately unexplored, as both Arjun and Riya recognized the fragility of altering the dynamics that had defined their success.

In the midst of their shared visions and uncharted emotions, Arjun and Riya continued to navigate the ever-evolving landscape of their collaboration. As they painted their canvas of change, they also acknowledged the canvas of their hearts—a masterpiece still waiting to be fully revealed. The journey, with all its twists and turns, held the promise of discovering what lay beyond the unspoken, a terrain of emotions yet to be explored.

"

Listen to destiny's whispers,
follow your passion, and let
belief in your journey guide you
to your life's purpose

"

3

The Crossroads of Life

June 17, 2021

Navigating the Storm

Arjun's journey of self-discovery led him to a profound realization—he needed to recalibrate his approach to life and work. The quest for success had, in many ways, overshadowed the core values that defined him. Inspired by the wisdom shared by Mr. Kapoor, Arjun embraced a new perspective on success—one that encompassed fulfillment, balance, and personal happiness.

As he immersed himself in the world of mindfulness and personal growth, Arjun began to integrate these principles into his daily life. He learned to appreciate the power of a well-balanced routine, incorporating moments of mindfulness and self-reflection amidst the demands of his professional responsibilities. This newfound equilibrium gradually became a source of strength, helping him navigate the challenges of the corporate world with greater resilience.

Arjun's transformation did not go unnoticed. His colleagues observed a subtle shift in his demeanor—a calmness that replaced the frenetic energy of the past. Intrigued by the change, some began to seek his advice on achieving a similar sense of balance in their own lives. Arjun, now not just a marketing professional but a beacon of mindfulness, willingly shared his insights.

In the midst of this personal evolution, Arjun's work at the marketing agency took on a new dimension. Fueled by a renewed sense of purpose, he initiated projects that aligned more closely with his values. Campaigns focused on social impact, sustainability, and human-centric marketing became his forte. The agency, initially skeptical of this shift, soon recognized the unique value Arjun brought to the table.

One day, as Arjun presented a groundbreaking campaign proposal, the room fell silent. The concept, woven with threads of empathy and authenticity, resonated deeply with both clients and colleagues. The campaign, aptly named "Heartstrings," aimed to evoke genuine emotions and connections, challenging the conventional notion of marketing.

The success of "Heartstrings" marked a turning point in Arjun's career. It was not just a triumph for the agency but a testament to the transformative power of aligning personal values with professional endeavors. Arjun's journey, from the chaos of corporate pressures to the tranquility of self-discovery, became an inspiring narrative within the industry.

As Arjun stood at another crossroads, he realized that the journey was an ongoing process—one of continuous growth, adaptation, and alignment with one's true self. He carried the lessons of mindfulness, balance, and purpose with him, knowing that success, in its most meaningful form, was a reflection of inner fulfillment. And so, with a heart aligned with his values, Arjun continued to navigate the dynamic landscape of marketing, a beacon of authenticity in a world often driven by external expectations.

During his journey of self-exploration, Arjun's encounters with diverse landscapes and cultures fueled not only his personal growth but also a profound shift in his perspective on the role of marketing in society. His sabbatical became a transformative pilgrimage, where the pages of his journal documented not only his reflections but also the stories of the people he met and the places he discovered.

In the Himalayas, surrounded by towering peaks and ancient monasteries, Arjun found inspiration in the simplicity of life. The teachings of mindfulness he had embraced in Bangalore took on a deeper resonance, and he began to envision a marketing approach rooted in authenticity and genuine connection.

On the beaches of Goa, where the rhythm of the waves echoed in his soul, Arjun contemplated the impact of marketing on consumer behavior. He realized the potential to influence not just purchasing decisions but also attitudes and values. This revelation became a cornerstone of his evolving philosophy—one that emphasized responsibility and ethical considerations in marketing practices.

The backwaters of Kerala, with their serene beauty and interconnected communities, became a canvas for Arjun's reflections on collaboration. He recognized the power of collective efforts and saw an opportunity for marketers to collaborate with communities, amplifying their voices and addressing social challenges.

Arjun's volunteer work in rural schools exposed him to the transformative power of education. It ignited a passion within him to leverage marketing not only for commercial success but also to support educational initiatives and empower marginalized communities.

As his sabbatical unfolded, Arjun's perspective on marketing underwent a metamorphosis. He realized that the essence of marketing lay not just in selling products but in telling stories that resonated with people's hearts and contributed to positive societal change.

Armed with this newfound purpose, Arjun returned from his journey, his backpack laden not only with memories but also with a vision for a different kind of marketing—a marketing that prioritized authenticity, social impact, and ethical practices. He re-entered the corporate world with a mission—to be a catalyst for change within the industry.

Arjun's colleagues, initially perplexed by his transformed outlook, soon recognized the value of his approach. His passion for social causes infused a fresh energy into the workplace. Together with like-minded colleagues, Arjun pioneered campaigns that not only promoted products but also supported community initiatives, environmental sustainability, and education.

In the ever-evolving landscape of marketing, Arjun became a trailblazer—a voice advocating for a more conscious and purpose-driven approach. His journey from the boardrooms of corporate marketing to the heartlands of India had not only shaped him but had also redefined his understanding of success and fulfillment. Arjun became a testament to the transformative power of self-discovery and the profound impact one individual could have in reshaping an entire industry.

These women, despite facing numerous challenges, had persevered and created a positive impact on their community. Arjun and Aisha were deeply moved by their story and decided to feature it prominently in the next edition of "The Changemakers."

The magazine's reach expanded, reaching not only urban readers but also those in rural areas. The stories became a source of inspiration for many, proving that change could start from any corner of the world. Arjun's dual role as a corporate marketer and a storyteller of change became a harmonious dance, each facet complementing the other.

"The Changemakers" continued to evolve, incorporating multimedia elements to make the stories more immersive. Short documentaries, podcasts, and social media campaigns became integral parts of their storytelling arsenal. Arjun and Aisha's collaboration became a testament to the transformative power of storytelling, proving that narratives could bridge gaps and create connections.

In the corporate sphere, Arjun's approach to marketing began to influence the industry. His campaigns at the marketing agency started to reflect a more socially conscious ethos. He advocated for sustainability, ethical practices, and community engagement, setting a new standard for marketing campaigns.

As "The Changemakers" garnered accolades and recognition, Arjun found himself at the center of a growing movement within the marketing community. Other professionals sought his guidance on how to infuse purpose into their work, and companies began reevaluating their strategies to align with a more meaningful and socially responsible approach.

Arjun's impact extended beyond the pages of the magazine. He became a speaker at conferences, sharing his insights on the intersection of marketing and social change. His journey, from the depths of corporate stress to the fulfillment of purpose-driven work, resonated with many aspiring marketers who sought a deeper connection between their careers and personal values.

In the midst of this success, Arjun and Aisha remained grounded, never losing sight of the core mission—to amplify the voices of those working for positive change. The storm of uncertainty that once clouded Arjun's path had transformed into a guiding light, illuminating a road paved with purpose and impact.

As they navigated the crossroads of life together, Arjun and Aisha knew that "The Changemakers" was more than a magazine; it was a movement, a catalyst for inspiring individuals to believe in the power of their stories and the change they could bring to the world.

The road ahead, filled with infinite possibilities, beckoned them to continue exploring, storytelling and making a difference—one narrative at a time.

Arjun and Aisha documented this transformative journey, capturing not just the economic progress but the sense of empowerment and pride radiating from the women and the entire village. The story became a testament to the incredible impact that collective effort, amplified by the right narrative, could have on a community.

The success of this campaign fueled Arjun and Aisha's commitment to using storytelling as a force for positive change. Their approach had transcended the boundaries of a conventional magazine and marketing agency; it had become a catalyst for tangible social impact.

As "The Changemakers" continued to gain momentum, Arjun and Aisha received invitations to speak at international forums and collaborate with organizations dedicated to social entrepreneurship. They realized that their journey had evolved beyond the pages of a magazine; it had become a movement that resonated with individuals and businesses around the world.

In the corporate arena, Arjun's influence continued to grow. His dual role as a marketer and a changemaker became a symbol of a new era in the industry—a shift toward purpose-driven marketing. Companies sought his guidance to align their strategies with ethical practices and community engagement, realizing that doing good could also be good for business.

Arjun and Aisha's collaborative efforts expanded beyond "The Changemakers." They initiated projects that aimed to bridge the gap between urban and rural communities, connecting consumers with the stories behind the products they purchased. Their vision of a more empathetic and interconnected world was gradually becoming a reality.

As their impact rippled through various sectors, Arjun and Aisha found fulfillment not just in the success of their projects but in the meaningful connections they forged along the way. Their journey, which began with a chance encounter and a shared vision, had become a testament to the transformative power of storytelling and purpose-driven collaboration.

In the end, Arjun and Aisha understood that the true measure of success was not just in personal achievements or industry recognition; it was in the positive change they inspired and the lives they touched. The road ahead, once uncertain, had unfolded into a landscape of endless possibilities, and they continued to navigate it together, driven by a shared commitment to creating a better, more compassionate world.

Arjun and Riya, an unlikely duo in the cutthroat world of marketing, discovered a shared passion that would redefine their lives and the industry itself. Their journey started at a marketing conference, where chance brought them together, and mentorship soon blossomed into a collaboration that transcended the conventional.

As they ventured into uncharted territory, Riya, the creative visionary, proposed a radical idea: to blur the lines between advertising and art. Their campaign, named "The Canvas of Change," aimed not only to sell a product but to ignite a cultural movement, weaving storytelling, visual art, and immersive experiences into the fabric of their strategy.

Arjun, drawn by Riya's vision, eagerly embraced the challenge. Together, they assembled a team of diverse talents, from artists to technologists, all driven by a shared passion for pushing marketing boundaries. "The Canvas of Change" took shape as an extraordinary project with a simple yet profound goal – to use art as a medium for stories of human resilience, compassion, and hope.

The first installation unveiled in Mumbai immersed visitors in the lives of underprivileged children striving for education. Life-sized portraits accompanied by stories of resilience allowed visitors to contribute messages of encouragement, transformed into art pieces for the children.

The campaign's success became a wildfire, sparking a cultural movement that reached global proportions. Amid media accolades, Arjun and Riya stayed true to their purpose, emphasizing the campaign's impact over personal recognition.

Their mentorship circle grew, and they devoted time to nurturing young marketers, passing on the wisdom gained through their journey. In the competitive realm of marketing, they became beacons of hope, proving that marketing could be a force for empathy, compassion, and social transformation.

In a joint talk, Arjun emphasized the power of marketers to shape culture and inspire positive change. Riya echoed his sentiments, urging marketers to be the change they wished to see in the world. Their philosophy earned them a place in marketing history textbooks.

As they delved into impactful campaigns, Arjun and Riya found time to explore new horizons. Their personalities, once confined to the boardroom, became a symphony of ideas, a harmony of personalities, and an unspoken understanding.

Their unexplored emotions added a layer of complexity to their relationship, a subtle tension that neither wanted to disrupt. Late nights at the office turned into shared laughter, moments when their connection shimmered with a different light.

The turning point came during a quiet street encounter. Beneath the moonlit sky, Riya voiced the unspoken question about the journey's destination. Arjun, acknowledging the uncharted territories, believed that the journey was more important than the destination.

Their connection, laden with unexplored emotions, set the stage for a journey of self-discovery and transformation. The chapters yet to be written held the promise of discovery and revealed a canvas of their hearts, a masterpiece still waiting to be fully revealed.

In this whirlwind of self-discovery, Arjun faced a crossroads in his corporate life. The pressures of the fast-paced environment had taken a toll on his well-being.

A conversation with his mentor, Mr. Kapoor, became a catalyst for self-reflection.

Life, Mr. Kapoor explained, was a journey of crossroads. At each juncture, one faced choices that shaped destiny. Arjun, realizing he had lost sight of his inner compass, embarked on a journey of self-exploration.

During this inward journey, Arjun rediscovered his love for writing, an art he had abandoned in pursuit of corporate success. Nature became his muse, long walks in Bangalore's lush parks offering clarity and purpose.

The turning point came as the sun set over Bangalore. Arjun, armed with a journal and a backpack, decided to take a sabbatical, traveling to the corners of India. In the mystical mountains of the Himalayas, serene beaches of Goa, and tranquil backwaters of Kerala, he immersed himself in local cultures, volunteering and learning.

This journey led Arjun to a profound realization — success was not just about external achievements but aligning actions with true self and values. As he documented stories of ordinary individuals making a difference, he met Aisha, a young photographer who shared his passion for storytelling.

Their collaboration gave birth to "The Changemakers," a digital magazine showcasing inspiring stories. The magazine's impact exceeded expectations, leading Arjun and Aisha to not only tell stories but actively contribute to change.

A story from a remote village, where women turned a handicraft venture into a thriving cooperative became a pivotal moment. Arjun and Aisha leveraged their marketing skills, creating an online store and launching a social media campaign. The response was overwhelming, transforming the lives of the women and their communities.

"The Changemakers" caught the attention of corporate partners and philanthropic organizations, leading to collaborations on impactful social campaigns. As Arjun and Aisha continued to navigate life's storms, they recognized the potential of storytelling and purpose-driven marketing.

Their journey, far from over, became a beacon of inspiration. Each story they shared aimed to inspire a new wave of changemakers, fostering compassion and empathy worldwide. Arjun and Aisha's unconventional collaboration, now a catalyst for change, continued to paint a canvas of positive impact.

As they looked ahead, Arjun and Aisha understood that life's crossroads were opportunities for exploration. Embracing challenges, discovering passions, and creating meaningful impacts were the essence of their journey. The adventure had just begun, with infinite possibilities waiting to be explored.

A Glimpse into "The Changemakers"

Maya's hands, weathered by the sun and sea, told tales of a life intricately linked to the rhythm of the tides.

Her story unfolded like a vivid tapestry, woven with threads of struggle, strength, and an unwavering connection to the ocean.

Arjun and Aisha, captivated by Maya's narrative, decided to dedicate an entire feature to her in "The Changemakers." They spent days immersed in her world, capturing the ebb and flow of her daily life through Aisha's lens and recording the cadence of her voice in Arjun's journal.

The coastal village became a backdrop for a profound story of resilience. Maya, along with other women in the village, had pioneered a sustainable fishing initiative. Their efforts not only preserved the marine ecosystem but also provided a source of steady income for the community.

As Maya cast her net into the sea, Arjun and Aisha witnessed the embodiment of a living metaphor — the interconnectedness of individual actions with the greater tapestry of community and nature. The images and words they captured painted a portrait of environmental stewardship and empowered women driving change.

The feature resonated deeply with "The Changemakers" audience. Maya's story became a catalyst for support, sparking a wave of interest and engagement. People from various corners of the world pledged their support for the fishing initiative, turning it into a symbol of hope and collaborative action.

Arjun and Aisha, humbled by the impact of their storytelling, realized that "The Changemakers" had evolved into more than a magazine. It had become a platform for amplifying voices that echoed positive change, a catalyst for building bridges of empathy between diverse communities.

Inspired by Maya's tale, Arjun and Aisha continued their exploration, seeking stories that showcased the resilience of the human spirit. They ventured into the arid landscapes of Rajasthan, where a community had transformed desert land into fertile farms using innovative water conservation methods.

The colors of Rajasthan, vibrant and bold, mirrored the spirit of the community. Arjun's words and Aisha's visuals captured the essence of transformation — a barren land now teeming with life. The feature unfolded like a chapter of hope, demonstrating the power of sustainable practices in the face of adversity.

"The Changemakers" garnered attention not only for its impactful stories but also for its innovative approach to storytelling. Arjun and Aisha experimented with immersive experiences, combining virtual reality and augmented reality to transport readers into the heart of the narratives.

Their journey through the lens of "The Changemakers" had become a celebration of diversity, resilience, and the collective potential for positive change. Arjun and Aisha stood at the helm of a storytelling revolution, steering the narrative towards a future where empathy and compassion bridged gaps and inspired action.

As the magazine's influence grew, Arjun and Aisha found themselves at the center of a community of changemakers — individuals and organizations united by a shared belief in the transformative power of storytelling. Collaborations flourished, giving rise to campaigns that addressed societal issues ranging from education to healthcare.

The impact of "The Changemakers" extended far beyond the digital pages. It materialized in tangible change, in communities empowered by the stories, and in readers who became active contributors to the causes they championed.

Arjun and Aisha's journey, initially guided by a shared vision, had morphed into a movement. The threads of purpose and passion they wove into the tapestry of "The Changemakers" connected hearts and minds across the globe. The magazine's legacy became a testament to the potential of storytelling as a force for positive transformation.

As they stood amidst the bustling city of Bangalore, where it all began, Arjun and Aisha recognized that their journey was a continuum. The tapestry they had woven together was vibrant, ever-expanding, and rich with the untold stories that awaited discovery.

The city's energy, once a backdrop, now resonated with the echoes of the stories they had shared. Arjun's analytical mind and Aisha's intuitive creativity had not only formed a powerful partnership but had also sparked a movement that transcended the boundaries of traditional storytelling.

Arjun and Aisha, as the architects of change, embraced the evolving chapters of their journey. With every story they uncovered, with every collaborative campaign they initiated, they painted strokes on the canvas of a world where positive change was not just a possibility but a collective reality.

The bustling city, the coastal village, the arid landscapes — each setting became a stage for narratives that echoed the universal human experience. Arjun and Aisha, through "The Changemakers," had not only told stories but had become storytellers of change, inspiring a global community to weave their threads into the collective tapestry of a better world.

Amidst the bustling city of Bangalore, a tapestry of two unique lives was being woven together with the threads of purpose and passion. Arjun and Aisha's journey into the world of "The Changemakers" had taken on a life of its own, revealing the intricacies of their partnership and the impact of their storytelling crusade.

Their collaboration was more than just a fusion of marketing skills and photography prowess; it was a meeting of kindred spirits, each bringing their individual strengths to the table. Arjun's analytical mind and strategic thinking found their counterpart in Aisha's intuitive creativity and visual storytelling.

As they delved deeper into their mission, the streets of Bangalore became more than just avenues of transit.

Each corner, each alley, seemed to hold stories waiting to be unearthed. The city's vibrant energy mirrored their own, propelling them forward on their shared journey.

Arjun's transition from the corporate world had been a leap into the unknown, a journey guided by the compass of his heart. From the moment he woke up to the aroma of chai and the warm embrace of sunlight, he was reminded that life had taken on a new rhythm. The corporate shackles had been replaced by the freedom of creative exploration.

His journal, once a repository of marketing strategies and to-do lists, had transformed into a repository of emotions and insights. The blank pages were now a canvas onto which he painted his dreams, his aspirations, and his vision for "The Changemakers." Every stroke of his pen was an affirmation of his commitment to stories that moved the soul.

Aisha's camera lens was her window to the world, capturing emotions and moments that words alone could not convey. Her photography was a dance of light and shadow, an intricate tapestry woven with the threads of life's intricacies. With each click, she breathed life into narratives that transcended the boundaries of language.

Their first encounter had been serendipitous, a convergence of paths at an art gallery where Aisha's photography exhibition was on display. The images spoke of untold stories, of emotions that ran deep and dreams that soared high. Their conversation flowed effortlessly, shifting from art to life, and in that instant, the seed of "The Changemakers" was sown.

Their journey took them to the heart of communities across India. From remote villages nestled in the embrace of nature to bustling urban landscapes, they sought stories that resonated with the pulse of humanity. With each adventure, anticipation hung in the air like a melody waiting to be played.

One such chapter of their journey unfolded in a coastal village in Kerala. The salty tang of the sea breeze greeted them as they arrived, carrying with it the echoes of laughter and resilience. It was here that they met Maya, a fisherwoman whose eyes held the wisdom of ages and the sparkle of determination.

Maya's hands, weathered by the sun and sea, told tales of a life intricately linked to the rhythm of the tides. Her story unfolded like a vivid tapestry woven with threads of struggle, strength, and an unwavering connection to the ocean.

Arjun and Aisha, captivated by Maya's narrative, decided to dedicate an entire feature to her in "The Changemakers." They spent days immersed in her world, capturing the ebb and flow of her daily life through Aisha's lens and recording the cadence of her voice in Arjun's journal.

The coastal village became a backdrop for a profound story of resilience. Maya, along with other women in the village, had pioneered a sustainable fishing initiative.

Their efforts not only preserved the marine ecosystem but also provided a source of steady income for the community.

As Maya cast her net into the sea, Arjun and Aisha witnessed the embodiment of a living metaphor — the interconnectedness of individual actions with the greater tapestry of community and nature. The images and words they captured painted a portrait of environmental stewardship and empowered women driving change.

The feature resonated deeply with "The Changemakers" audience. Maya's story became a catalyst for support, sparking a wave of interest and engagement. People from various corners of the world pledged their support for the fishing initiative, turning it into a symbol of hope and collaborative action.

Arjun and Aisha, humbled by the impact of their storytelling, realized that "The Changemakers" had evolved into more than a magazine. It had become a platform for amplifying voices that echoed positive change, a catalyst for building bridges of empathy between diverse communities.

Inspired by Maya's tale, Arjun and Aisha continued their exploration, seeking stories that showcased the resilience of the human spirit. They ventured into the arid landscapes of Rajasthan, where a community had transformed desert land into fertile farms using innovative water conservation methods.

The colors of Rajasthan, vibrant and bold, mirrored the spirit of the community. Arjun's words and Aisha's visuals captured the essence of transformation — a barren land now teeming with life. The feature unfolded like a chapter of hope, demonstrating the power of sustainable practices in the face

As the canvas of their collaboration expanded, Arjun and Aisha stood at the crossroads of possibility and potential. Their journey with "The Changemakers" was a testament to the extraordinary impact that could be achieved when a shared vision was nurtured with dedication and love. And as they stood on the threshold of the unknown, they knew that the path ahead was illuminated by the stories yet to be shared, the lives yet to be touched, and the change yet to be ignited.

"

Facing problems, learning from mistakes, and never giving up leads to overcoming the toughest storms of life.

"

4

Embracing the Unknown

July 11, 2021

In the intricate tapestry of Arjun's existence, the interweaving threads of marketing prowess and fervent advocacy for change created a labyrinthine path that demanded an artful balance. On one side sprawled the bustling expanse of corporate demands—a realm pulsating with the rhythm of targets, deadlines, and the unyielding cadence of competition. On the opposing frontier, bathed in the soft glow of hope, stretched the domain of "The Changemakers," a canvas adorned with hues of empathy, compassion, and an unwavering dedication to societal transformation.

As Arjun traversed this precarious tightrope, he confronted challenges that weren't mere obstacles but profound crucibles shaping his character. The corporate realm, with its alluring promises of recognition and financial ascension, tugged at him, tempting him toward the siren call of conventional success. Concurrently, the gratification derived from storytelling and its profound impact on societal change resonated within him—an incessant echo that reverberated at the very core of his being.

This journey, however, was far from a stroll in the park. With "The Changemakers" rapidly ascending to international prominence, its readership burgeoned into a global tapestry of changemakers, activists, and philanthropists. Yet, this surge in popularity brought with it a cascade of logistical complexities. Arjun and Aisha, the dynamic architects behind the magazine, found themselves grappling with a torrent of responsibilities— ranging from the curation of thought-provoking content to the meticulous maintenance of a digital sanctuary for their readers. All the while, they navigated the intricate tapestry of forging connections within a diverse and expansive global community.

In the tempest of challenges, a transformative moment unfolded. Arjun's inbox received an email from Rahul, a devoted reader of "The Changemakers." A young marketing professional, Rahul not only pledged his skills but also his fervor for change. Gratitude surged within Arjun as he embraced Rahul's entry into the team.

Yet, Rahul's impact exceeded the realm of skill contribution. His perspective brought a breath of fresh air, his enthusiasm reignited a dormant vigor, and his steadfast commitment ignited the collective flame of change. Under his guidance, the team burgeoned, molding "The Changemakers" into a dynamic platform that transcended the digital sphere. It now encompassed events, workshops, and immersive sessions, effectively bridging the gap between readers and the celebrated changemakers.

In the ebb and flow of triumphs and trials, a profound shift occurred in Arjun's leadership style. Recognizing the power of collaborative efforts, he cultivated an atmosphere of inclusivity, where each team member's achievement resonated as a collective triumph. The dichotomy between corporate aspirations and his passion for storytelling gradually dissolved, making way for a harmonious synthesis that thrived on the impact of collective endeavors.

Amidst transformative currents, restlessness stirred within Arjun—a lingering question of how to magnify his impact. This question found its answer during a visit to a humble rural village. Here, he encountered a group of spirited young girls brimming with dreams but confined by the constraints of limited resources. The idea crystallized: education held the power to transform lives, igniting the fires of empowerment.

With this revelation, "Education for All" was born. Arjun harnessed his marketing prowess to orchestrate campaigns that resonated with hearts, rallying support to offer scholarships and educational resources to underprivileged children. A network coalesced, fueled by a shared passion for change. The response was overwhelming—individuals, unified by empathy, stepped forward, contributing time, funds, and expertise. The initiative's tendrils spread to remote villages and underserved communities, a testament to the potential of collective action.

Witnessing the palpable transformation kindled by "Education for All," Arjun's purpose crystallized. His journey was no longer a balancing act; it was a harmonious dance of converging passions. "The Changemakers" and "Education for All" merged seamlessly—a testament to his commitment to empower individuals and forge a more compassionate world.

And so, the circular arc of Arjun's journey unfolded. From the crossroads of uncertainty emerged a profound realization—life was not about navigating divergent paths but about converging them into a force for good. The tightrope transformed into a conduit of change, each step a testament to his unwavering dedication to creating a legacy of impact.

As Arjun gazed ahead, the path revealed itself—a journey adorned with trials, triumphs, and the promise of transformation. Armed with the alchemy of storytelling and fortified by the strength of collaboration, he embarked on a quest to leave an indelible mark upon the world.

The odyssey persisted, every stride a testament to Arjun's steadfast commitment to shaping narratives of change—one story at a time. Dancing with the enigmatic threads of destiny in this journey, Arjun comprehended that the most profound chapters were still waiting to be penned.

Rediscovering the Inner Rhythms

In the bustling metropolis of Mumbai, where the cacophony of car horns and city life drowned out the symphony of the soul, lived Arjun, a middle-aged man at a crossroads in life. Two decades entrenched in the corporate machinery had granted him success, yet within the relentless rhythm of his daily routine, he'd become a mere spectator in the grand theatre of his own existence.

One rainy evening, the city lights reflected off the wet streets, creating a mesmerizing dance of illumination. Arjun, feeling an inexplicable pull, found himself drawn into a small, unassuming bookstore nestled between towering structures. The air inside, heavy with the comforting scent of aged pages, wrapped around him like a warm embrace. Soft murmurs of countless stories seemed to beckon him into a world where forgotten dreams could be rekindled and the mundane transformed into the extraordinary.

The shelves, adorned with books that held the wisdom of centuries, invited exploration. Amongst them, "The Changemakers" stood out—a mosaic of faces depicted on the cover, each telling tales of metamorphosis and profound impact. As Arjun turned the pages, he felt the rhythmic pulse of inspiration, like a heartbeat echoing through the very core of his being.

The stories within were not mere narratives; they were living chronicles of ordinary individuals transcending the ordinary. They were teachers awakening the minds of the young, activists fighting passionately for justice, entrepreneurs sculpting sustainable futures, and artists wielding their craft to raise awareness. In the quiet moments of reading, Arjun found a reflection of his own dormant dreams and aspirations, like forgotten treasures waiting to be rediscovered.

In the embrace of the rain-soaked city and the profound wisdom within those pages, Arjun sensed a call, not just to read but to live. It wasn't merely a book; it was a catalyst for the reawakening of his inner voice, urging him to break free from the invisible chains of conformity that had bound him for too long.

As the rain continued to tap rhythmically on the windows of the bookstore, Arjun's heart resonated with the gentle melody of possibility. The bookstore, once a refuge from the rain, had become a sanctuary for the storm within him. Each word he absorbed, each story he internalized, was a drop of inspiration, slowly eroding the barriers that had confined his true self.

In that quiet space, amidst the pages and the rain, Arjun's journey began—a journey to rediscover the essence of who he truly was. The bookstore became his haven, and "The Changemakers" his guide. With every step he took, he could feel the symphony of his own soul-stirring, harmonizing with the melody of purpose that had long been silenced.

And so, as the city outside continued its chaotic dance, Arjun embarked on a dance of his own—a dance with the forgotten tunes of his dreams, a dance that would lead him from the mundane to the extraordinary, from the corporate machinery to the beating heart of his true calling.

That night, Arjun found no solace in sleep, the stirrings of contemplation keeping him restless until the dawn broke its first rays. In the quiet unfolding of the morning, a decision crystallized within him - he was poised to embark on a transformative journey, a quest for self-discovery and reinvention. His destination: the realm of changemakers, where he hoped to discover the elusive pieces completing his personal puzzle.

Empowered by a newfound sense of purpose, Arjun ventured into a world pulsating with social impact and change-making. Workshops, conferences, and networking events became the waypoints of his journey, each interaction weaving a thread into the tapestry of his unfolding narrative. Activists, social entrepreneurs, educators, and artists unfolded their unique stories before him, each tale a stepping stone on his path.

Among the first changemakers to captivate Arjun was Aisha, a vibrant soul steering a non-profit dedicated to empowering underprivileged children through education and the arts. Her passion, like a contagious flame, ignited a fire within Arjun, and her steadfast belief in the potency of change became a beacon for his own aspirations.

In the cozy ambiance of a cafe, Aisha shared her tale of resilience and determination, a narrative woven with the threads of challenges faced, obstacles conquered, and countless lives touched. For Aisha, change-making transcended profession—it was an inseparable facet of her existence.

Arjun marveled at the simplicity inherent in Aisha's approach to change-making. She championed the belief that change was born from modest, deliberate actions, emphasizing the potential of every individual to make a difference, no matter how seemingly inconsequential. Her words resonated with him, awakening a spark of hope and limitless potential.

Over the ensuing months, Arjun delved deeper into the realm of changemakers, forging meaningful connections and immersing himself in a diverse ecosystem. It became evident that each individual and organization played a distinctive role in the collective endeavor to craft a better world.

One of the most impactful encounters unfolded with Vikram, a visionary social entrepreneur who had ingeniously developed technology to deliver clean drinking water to remote villages. Vikram's palpable passion for sustainability and social impact left an indelible mark on Arjun, and his unwavering commitment to harnessing technology for the greater good resonated deeply.

As Arjun ventured further into the vibrant tapestry of changemakers, a profound shift occurred in his perception of the world. He began to discern the invisible threads connecting all living beings, recognizing the intricate interconnectedness of humanity and the cascading effects of every action.

The revelation struck him: change-making transcended grand gestures or heroic acts. It was a dance of vulnerability, an intentional progression of small steps, a harmonious blend of surrender and action. It entailed releasing the ego's hunger for recognition and embracing the joy found in service.

Arjun's understanding of success underwent a metamorphosis. He came to realize that true success wasn't quantified by external achievements or material wealth. Instead, it resided in the profound impact one could have on the lives of others. The changemakers he encountered found fulfillment not in accolades or possessions but in the knowledge that their actions were contributing to a positive transformation in the world.

In his ongoing journey of self-discovery, Arjun shed the layers of his old identity. Liberated from the shackles of societal expectations, he embraced the uncertainty of the path he was forging. No longer confined to predefined molds, he reveled in the freedom of authenticity.

With each encounter, Arjun's purpose crystallized. He discovered his calling as a storyteller—his mission is to amplify the voices of the changemakers, to share their inspiring narratives with the world, and to ignite the spark of positive change in others.

And so, with a heart brimming with gratitude and determination, Arjun inaugurated a new chapter of his life. Armed with the potent tool of storytelling and the profound wisdom of the changemakers, he embarked on creating a platform. This platform, named "The Changemakers," surpassed the realm of a mere magazine. It burgeoned into a movement—a collective of ordinary individuals accomplishing extraordinary feats, a beacon of hope and endless possibility, and a force of collective impact.

In the subsequent chapter of his journey, Arjun unravels the profound influence of creative expression and the enchanting beauty found in embracing vulnerability. Becoming a storyteller, he would discover his voice, unlocking a symphony within that promised not only to transform his own life but to resonate through the lives of countless others.

With every passing day, as Arjun delved deeper into the tapestry of changemakers, a metamorphosis swept over him. It was as though he meticulously peeled away layers of his former self, revealing a new, more authentic iteration. The cocoon of transformation enveloped him, and he emerged, wings unfurled, into the boundless possibilities of his newfound identity.

His engagements with the changemakers had a profound impact on his outlook on life. The narratives of resilience, courage, and unwavering dedication reached into the recesses of his heart, weaving threads of inspiration in ways he hadn't anticipated. Arjun found himself in introspection, contemplating his own journey, the pivotal choices he had made, and the unique path he had traversed.

One evening, as he sat by the window, captivated by the city lights below, Arjun experienced a surge of emotions. The realization dawned on him that he could no longer settle for the status quo and no longer find contentment in mere existence. A profound desire welled within him—an aspiration to carve a meaningful niche in the world, to imprint a positive legacy that would endure beyond his own lifetime.

Aisha's resonant words reverberated in his mind - "Change starts with small, intentional actions." Arjun internalized this wisdom, understanding that impactful change need not be grandiose. The journey could commence within his immediate sphere of influence, guided by the principles of empathy, compassion, and service.

As Arjun immersed himself further in the realm of changemakers, he found himself drawn to the transformative potential of storytelling. Recognizing the profound ability of stories to traverse boundaries and forge deep emotional connections between individuals, he resolved to channel his fervor for change into a new venture—an endeavor that would elevate the voices of those weaving extraordinary impacts.

"The Changemakers" was conceived from Arjun's earnest desire to share the narratives of ordinary individuals effecting extraordinary change. He invested his heart and soul into the project, reaching out to changemakers across diverse landscapes. The responses flooded in, a testament to the immense reservoir of stories waiting to be told—teachers who had revolutionized their classrooms, activists who had mobilized communities for change, and entrepreneurs who had woven businesses with a social conscience.

With each narrative he gathered, Arjun experienced a profound renewal of purpose. His role extended beyond that of a mere storyteller; he saw himself as a catalyst for change. His ambition went beyond the recounting of tales — he aspired to create a ripple effect, motivating others to take action, no matter how modest. However, with the expansion of the platform came burgeoning challenges. Arjun found himself navigating the intricate balance between his corporate responsibilities and his burgeoning passion. There were nights when he toiled ceaselessly, propelled by his unwavering determination to make a meaningful impact. It was during one such night that he received an unexpected message from a reader.

The message originated from a young woman named Maya, who had stumbled upon "The Changemakers" and was profoundly moved by the narratives she discovered. Maya opened up about her own aspiration to establish a community library in her neighborhood—a haven where children could access books and embark on journeys through the world of knowledge.

Arjun found himself deeply moved by Maya's vision and boundless enthusiasm. In her dream, he recognized an opportunity to bridge the divide between the virtual world of storytelling and the tangible impact on the ground. With conviction, he resolved to collaborate with Maya, throwing his support behind her to bring this shared dream to fruition.

Their partnership marked an evolution in Arjun's journey. No longer confined to the realm of narrating stories, he actively engaged in the change he aspired to inspire. Shoulder to shoulder with Maya, they mobilized the community, garnered funds, and materialized the dream of a community library. The sheer joy radiating from the children's faces as they held books in their hands served as a tangible testament to the potency of collective action.

As Arjun reflected on his odyssey, he acknowledged the vast distance traveled from the man who once felt adrift in the monotony of corporate life. Along the way, he had rediscovered the cadence of his inner self, his purpose, and his connection to a broader tapestry of change.

The symphony of his life, once drowned out by the cacophony of routine, now harmonized with the melodies of compassion, service, and impact. Standing at the crossroads of his transformed existence, Arjun recognized that this was merely the inception of a beautiful journey—a journey where each step was a note in the symphony of change, creating a melody destined to resonate through the annals of time.

In the denouement, Arjun's story stood as a testament to the potency of embracing the unknown, heeding the whispers of the heart, and daring to make a difference. Peering into the expanse of possibilities that lay ahead, he realized his symphony of change was poised for composition—one transformative note at a time.

Amidst the rich tapestry of stories, Arjun's own narrative underwent a profound transformation. Encounters with changemakers had kindled a flame within him, but it was the dialogues that bestowed depth and vibrancy upon his journey.

One evening, as the sun dipped below the horizon, casting a warm golden glow over the city, Arjun found himself in a quaint café with Aisha. The aroma of freshly brewed coffee enveloped them as they exchanged dreams, fears, and aspirations.

Aisha's eyes gleamed with enthusiasm as she recounted the challenges of initiating her non-profit organization. "There were days when it felt overwhelming," she conceded, a wistful smile gracing her lips. "But every time I looked into the eyes of a child whose life we had touched, I knew it was worth it."

Arjun listened intently, captivated not just by Aisha's words but by the fervor radiating from her every expression. Her narrative epitomized the resilience and unwavering belief in a cause.

Turning the spotlight on Arjun, Aisha posed a question that cut through the ambient warmth of the café, "And what about you? What prompted your journey into changemakers?"

Arjun's gaze wandered as if seeking the right words amidst the labyrinth of his thoughts. "I suppose I had forgotten why I ventured into the world of marketing initially," he confessed. "I got entangled in the pursuit of success, and along the way, I lost touch with the impact I originally sought to create."

Aisha's hand extended across the table, settling gently on Arjun's. "You're not alone in that," her reassurance enveloped him. "We all lose our way at times. But the beauty lies in finding our way back, in rediscovering the essence of who we are."

As they sat there, hands intertwined across the table, Arjun sensed a connection that transcended verbal expression. It was a communion of shared purpose, two individuals intertwining their narratives in pursuit of a common goal.

With the deepening of their friendship, Arjun found himself engrossed in conversations with other changemakers. He delved into the intricacies of Vikram's sustainable technology, witnessed the unwavering dedication of educators reshaping lives through education, and marveled at the compassion of artists leveraging their craft to amplify awareness of social issues.

Each dialogue carved a new layer of understanding within Arjun's heart. He recognized that the journey of a changemaker was neither linear nor devoid of doubts. Uncertainty loomed at times, self-doubt crept in, and the weight of responsibility occasionally felt almost unbearable.

Yet, amidst these challenges, a common thread of unwavering determination emerged. Arjun heard it in the teacher's words, describing the joy of seeing a student's eyes light up with understanding. He felt it in the stories of individuals who had triumphed over personal struggles to instigate positive change in their communities.

One conversation etched an indelible mark on Arjun's soul, and it was with a young force named Riya. A fervent environmentalist, she had spearheaded a campaign to illuminate the perils of plastic pollution. Riya's eyes blazed with unwavering conviction as she articulated her mission to safeguard the planet for generations to come.

"It's not easy," Riya confessed, vulnerability lacing her voice. "There are days when I feel like I'm waging a losing battle, especially when I witness those around me unconsciously contributing to plastic use."

Arjun observed Riya, her determination radiating despite the challenges. "You've already accomplished so much," he assured her. "You've heightened awareness, ignited change, and initiated crucial conversations. Remember, even the smallest ripple can birth a wave of transformation."

As their gazes locked, Arjun discerned a reflection of his own journey mirrored in Riya's trials and triumphs. He realized that the path of change-making wasn't solitary; it was a collective odyssey where individuals converged, shared their stories, and provided support through the peaks and valleys.

In the realm of conversations and connections, Arjun's journey continued to unfurl. Each dialogue bestowed fresh insights, alternative perspectives, and a profound comprehension of the formidable power inherent in human connection. He gleaned that change-making transcended the act of creating impact; it was a metamorphosis of oneself in the intricate dance of transformation.

The café lights dimmed, casting a subtle glow as the evening seamlessly transitioned into night. Arjun and Aisha lingered in conversation, their voices weaving into the gentle hum of the city beyond. In this fleeting moment, enveloped by tales of transformation and the comforting embrace of camaraderie, Arjun felt an undeniable certainty – he was precisely where he was destined to be. On this journey of exploration, guided by conversations that served as luminous beacons illuminating the path forward.

The Connection Within

Arjun's foray into the realm of changemakers unfolded as a transformative odyssey, awakening a dormant fire within him. Immersed in their narratives, he began to perceive the world through a new lens—one tinted with compassion, purpose, and an unwavering belief in the potency of collective action.

Among the myriad changemakers he encountered, Aisha's unwavering determination held a magnetic allure for Arjun. The memory of the day they had shared a cozy cafe lingered vividly, the fragrance of freshly brewed coffee intermingling with the scent of hope that permeated the air.

In that intimate setting, Aisha's eyes emanated a rare amalgamation of passion and serenity as she unfolded her journey. Her voice, tinged with emotion, resonated through the cozy space as she recounted the challenges of building her nonprofit organization. "There were days when I felt like giving up," she admitted, her gaze fixed on a distant horizon. "But then I would think of those children—their eyes filled with dreams despite their circumstances. That's what kept me going."

Arjun found himself captivated by the authenticity of Aisha's narrative. Her story stood as a testament to the indomitable power of resilience, striking a profound chord within him. It was as if a connection had been forged between their souls, their paths destined to intersect and catalyze each other's journeys.

With each interaction, Arjun's comprehension of change-making underwent a profound evolution. It dawned on him that this endeavor wasn't merely about resolving surface-level issues; it was a process of delving into the underlying dynamics, addressing concerns at their roots. He bore witness to changemakers engaging in meaningful dialogues with communities, attuning themselves to the needs of the people, and co-creating solutions that were not only sustainable but also empowering.

One evening, as the sun dipped below the horizon, painting the sky in a tapestry of orange and gold, Arjun found himself in the company of Vikram, a social entrepreneur deeply committed to environmental sustainability. Their conversation unfolded within Vikram's unassuming yet impactful workspace, surrounded by prototypes of water purification systems and intricate diagrams detailing the workings of his innovative creations.

"I firmly believe that every problem carries its own solution within," Vikram asserted, his eyes ablaze with conviction. "The key is unlocking that solution through innovation and collaboration." As Vikram spoke, Arjun sensed the seamless fusion of science and empathy propelling Vikram's work. It was a symphony of intellect and heart—a melody resonating with the core of Arjun's being.

In the ensuing weeks, Arjun's personal journey of self-discovery mirrored the changing seasons. Just as nature shed its old leaves to make way for new growth, Arjun discarded layers of doubt and complacency that had hindered his progress. In every conversation, every story, and every connection forged, he unearthed a renewed sense of purpose.

As Arjun's comprehension deepened, he dared to step beyond the confines of his comfort zone. Workshops beckoned him, where the realms of technology and social change converged. Innovators deliberated on the potential of artificial intelligence and data analytics as forces for the greater good.

A particular dialogue from one such workshop lingered in Arjun's mind, spoken by a young technologist, "Technology is a tool, and its impact is determined by how we wield it. We have the power to use it for surveillance and control, or we can harness it to democratize information and empower marginalized communities."

These words reverberated within Arjun long after the workshop's conclusion. He grasped that the same principle applied to his role as a storyteller. A choice lay before him – to wield his words in perpetuating the status quo or amplifying the voices challenging it.

Arjun's writing became a conduit for change. He crafted stories transcending geographical boundaries, tales celebrating the triumph of the human spirit over adversity. Through his words, readers traversed remote villages, bustling urban centers, and untouched landscapes, immersing themselves in the untold stories of those often overlooked.

Yet, as Arjun poured his heart onto the pages, he confronted the shadows dormant within him. To narrate stories of transformation, he recognized the need to face his own fears and vulnerabilities. Embracing the concealed facets of himself became a requisite step in his journey.

The process proved to be both cathartic and challenging for Arjun. Moments of doubt would creep in, questioning his qualification to tell these transformative stories. He turned to Aisha, confiding in her with the same vulnerability he encouraged in his writing.

Aisha's response served as a gentle reminder that vulnerability was the crucible of connection. "Arjun," she reassured, her voice a soothing balm, "it's okay to feel uncertain. What matters is your intention – the intention to illuminate stories that inspire change. Your words possess the power to spark conversations, and conversations, in turn, have the power to ignite movements."

Aisha's words resonated with Arjun on a profound level. He understood that having all the answers wasn't necessary; what mattered was a willingness to pose the right questions and listen with an open heart. Guided by Aisha's wisdom and fortified by his own inner resolve,

Arjun delved even deeper into stories with the potential to reshape perspectives and catalyze collective action.

As Arjun's commitment to his mission deepened, he underwent a profound shift in his own consciousness. He recognized that change-making wasn't merely a sequence of external actions; it constituted a journey of inner transformation. The symphony of change reverberating within him mirrored the evolution of his own self.

In the heart of the city's bustling streets, Arjun sought moments of serenity, places where he could reflect and commune with his innermost thoughts. A quiet park became his refuge, the gentle rustling of leaves and distant chatter providing a soothing backdrop to his contemplations.

During one such afternoon, he had an encounter that etched an indelible mark on his soul. Seated on a park bench, absorbed in his notebook, a young girl approached him. She couldn't have been more than ten years old, her eyes brimming with curiosity and her infectious smile radiating wonder.

"Are you a writer?" she asked, her innocence tinged with awe.

Arjun nodded, returning her smile. "Yes, I am."

The girl's eyes sparkled with excitement. "I want to be a writer too. I have stories to tell."

Her enthusiasm moved Arjun profoundly. He gently encouraged her to share her stories, and as she spoke, he realized that wisdom often emerged from the most unexpected sources. Her tales, simple yet profound, each carried a nugget of truth that resonated with his own journey.

"You know," she said, her voice a gentle whisper, "stories possess the power to evoke emotions – emotions people didn't know they could feel. They can alter the way people perceive the world."

Arjun was struck by the profound simplicity of her words. In that innocent exchange, he rediscovered that the heart of storytelling lay in its capacity to touch hearts and instigate change. It served as a prompt to strip away the intricacies and return to the essence of his craft – the simple act of sharing a story with the potential to transform lives.

Embracing this newfound clarity, Arjun's writing underwent a transformation. He started infusing his stories with unfiltered emotions, allowing his vulnerability to seep through the ink and onto the paper. He realized that his doubts and fears were not weaknesses to conceal but strengths to share. Through his words, he created a space for readers to connect with their own vulnerabilities and, in doing so, muster the courage to create change.

Yet, the path of a changemaker was not devoid of challenges. As Arjun continued to amplify the voices of the unheard, he encountered resistance from those entrenched in the status quo. An interaction with a skeptical journalist lingered in his memory.

The journalist questioned the impact of Arjun's work, stating, "You write inspiring stories, but how do you know they're making a real difference? How do you measure the impact of your words?"

Arjun paused, responding with unwavering conviction. "Change is often subtle, like the rustling of leaves before a storm. It may not always be quantifiable, but it's discernible in the hearts of those who read these stories and feel moved to take action. The impact is not always immediate; it's the seed that's planted and nurtured until it blooms."

At that moment, Arjun recognized that his work was a testament to the power of patience and persistence. Just as a seed needed time to germinate and grow, the impact of his stories might take time to manifest. Yet, he trusted in the process, understanding that change was a continuum transcending the confines of time and space.

Arjun's journey also led him to delve into the nuances of collaboration. He witnessed changemakers from diverse backgrounds coming together to create a greater impact than they could achieve alone. An indelible memory was his attendance at a roundtable discussion where activists, artists, scientists, and educators converged to address a complex issue plaguing their city.

As the conversation flowed, Arjun was struck by the diversity of perspectives. Each participant brought a unique lens through which to view the issue, and as they shared their insights, a tapestry of solutions began to emerge. It was a symphony of minds coming together, each note contributing to a harmonious melody of change.

Amidst the dialogue, Arjun found himself engrossed in a conversation with a climate scientist named Dr. Maya. She spoke about the interconnectedness of the planet's ecosystems and the delicate balance being disrupted by human activity.

"Our actions ripple through the fabric of the environment," Dr. Maya explained her expression a mix of concern and determination. "But just as we've caused harm, we also have the power to heal. It's about recognizing that we're not separate from nature; we're an integral part of it."

Her words resonated with Arjun, reaffirming his belief in the profound impact that collective action could have on the world. He realized that change-making was not a solitary endeavor; it was a collaborative symphony that required individuals to play their unique roles in harmony.

As the years unfolded, "The Changemakers Magazine" blossomed beyond Arjun's most ambitious expectations. It evolved into a dynamic force for change, motivating individuals from diverse backgrounds to venture beyond their comfort zones and make meaningful contributions.

66

Coincidences noticed changes embraced, fate trusted—this is where life's surprising magic unfolds

99

5

Threads of Resilience

October 1, 2021

The Unseen Threads

The sun dipped below the horizon, casting the evening sky in warm hues of orange and pink. Arjun sought solace on a well-worn bench nestled in a local park. As he observed the serene scene before him, his mind meandered through the intricate corridors of his thoughts. Several years had passed since he embarked on his transformative journey as a changemaker, and along the way, he witnessed a tapestry of courage, resilience, and hope woven by the hands of countless individuals. Yet, amid all the success and impact he facilitated, a subtle whisper of curiosity tugged at the corners of his consciousness – a whisper that hinted at the existence of hidden threads, threads connecting his past, present, and future in ways he was yet to fathom.

The gentle caress of a breeze rustled the leaves of the nearby trees, and a soft, melodious voice seemed to emanate from the wind itself, "Arjun, the dance of destiny has only just begun."

Arjun turned around, half-expecting to see someone there, yet the space remained empty. However, he couldn't shake the sensation that an unseen force was guiding him toward a new chapter in his life. An enigmatic energy swirled around him, igniting his curiosity and urging him to unravel the mystery that lay in wait. Eager to explore this new dimension of his journey, Arjun felt a rush of anticipation as he prepared to embark on a quest that would uncover the hidden threads intricately connecting his life's narrative.

He delved into the heart of his family history, seeking insight from the generations that had come before him. Conversations with his parents and grandparents unveiled stories of struggle and triumph, dreams and aspirations, and a legacy of resilience passed down through time. With each anecdote, Arjun felt a sense of kinship with those who had walked similar paths – a lineage of change agents whose footprints had left indelible marks on the fabric of history.

Amid the yellowed and timeworn pages of an ancient family album, Arjun unearthed a sepia-toned photograph, capturing the visage of his great-grandfather—a valiant freedom fighter who had gallantly battled for India's independence. The eyes immortalized in the frame glowed with an undying flame of resolve, and Arjun couldn't escape the profound connection he felt to the man whose blood ran through his own veins. It was as if the spirit of his great-grandfather lingered, an ethereal whisper urging him to grasp the torch of positive change and step confidently into the legacy bestowed upon him.

As Arjun delved deeper into his ancestral heritage, he stumbled upon a trove of letters meticulously crafted by his grandmother—an indomitable force in advocating for women's rights and a stalwart social worker. The ink on those pages resonated with fervor and unwavering belief, revealing to Arjun that the essence of change-making was intricately woven into the fabric of his lineage. He realized that his journey wasn't solitary; he was part of an unbroken chain of transformation, where individuals had wielded their agency to etch an enduring impact on the canvas of the world.

As he meticulously assembled the fragments of his familial mosaic, a kaleidoscope of interconnected patterns and synchronous events unfolded. It was as if the cosmos itself conspired to gently nudge him along a predetermined trajectory. The happenstance encounters that blossomed into profound connections, the serendipitous turns that altered the trajectory of his journey—all aligned with a cosmic design, propelling him purposefully toward a revelation waiting patiently to unfurl.

Yet, the persistent question lingered – what was his purpose? What intricate design had destiny woven for him? These inquiries tugged at Arjun's consciousness like an unsolved riddle, and he sensed that the answers were not confined to the boundaries of his individual experiences.

Embarking on a voyage of exploration, Arjun traversed diverse corners of the world, immersing himself in the rich tapestry of cultures and communities that painted the global landscape. His intention was clear: to gain a profound understanding of the world's people and their myriad stories, hoping that this understanding would cast light upon the path to his own purpose.

His travels took him across bustling metropolises, remote villages, and the diverse landscapes that spanned the spectrum in between. Along this journey, he encountered a captivating array of characters – artists and activists, entrepreneurs and educators – each carrying a unique narrative of change. Their stories resonated with him, providing glimpses into the universal themes of resilience, aspiration, and transformation. Through their struggles, he gleaned insights into the threads that wove humanity together, transcending geographical boundaries and cultural differences.

In the heart of Africa, Arjun crossed paths with a group of young women who had defied overwhelming odds to pursue education. Their indomitable spirit in the face of adversity struck a chord deep within him, prompting a commitment to support their cause by providing scholarships and resources for their studies. Witnessing their determination, he realized that the threads of his own purpose were intricately interwoven with the collective threads of empowerment and education.

In the majestic mountains of Nepal, Arjun encountered a community of farmers committed to sustainable agricultural practices, safeguarding their land and preserving their way of life. Their dedication to environmental stewardship left an indelible imprint on his soul. Collaborating with local NGOs, he championed the cause of sustainable farming techniques and raised awareness about the urgent need to address climate change. It was during these moments that he sensed the threads of his purpose weaving into the broader tapestry of global sustainability and environmental responsibility.

In the dynamic streets of Tokyo, Arjun engaged with a network of tech entrepreneurs utilizing innovation to address pressing societal issues. The creativity and ingenuity he encountered ignited a desire to create a platform uniting changemakers worldwide. Through these interactions, he discovered threads linking him to the realms of technology, collaboration, and the boundless potential of collective impact.

As he traversed continents, the realization dawned upon Arjun that his purpose was not a singular thread woven into a specific cause or locale. Instead, it was a vibrant tapestry spanning diverse landscapes, encompassing a spectrum of causes and people. His purpose was that of a bridge – connecting individuals, ideas, and resources across cultures and borders, catalyzing a global movement of changemakers. The profound understanding that his very identity was that of a citizen of the world, intricately tied to the threads of interconnectedness, washed over him with a sense of purpose and clarity.

Back in the comforting embrace of his hometown, Arjun found himself seated on the edge of his familiar bench, a newfound clarity settling within him. The threads of his past, the tales of his travels, and the whispers of his ancestors had converged into a tapestry of destiny uniquely his own. He recognized that the dance of destiny was not a solo performance; it was a collective symphony of threads woven together by countless hands, each thread contributing to the richness of the whole.

With this profound realization, Arjun felt a renewed sense of purpose and embarked on a mission to translate his insights into meaningful action. He conceived an audacious idea, one that would resonate across the globe, fostering connections among changemakers and amplifying their collective impact. It was time to weave a virtual tapestry, a tapestry of individuals united by a shared vision for positive change.

And so, "The Global Changemakers Network" was born—an innovative online platform designed to connect individuals and organizations from every corner of the world. It served as a digital hub where ideas were shared, resources were pooled, and collaborations were sparked. The network became a thriving ecosystem of changemakers, each thread contributing its unique hue to the vibrant tapestry of global transformation.

The response to the platform was nothing short of extraordinary. From bustling urban centers to remote villages, individuals from diverse backgrounds joined the network, sharing their stories and projects with fervor. Partnerships flourished, initiatives were launched, and the ripple effect of positive change resonated across continents.

Arjun's journey had come full circle. What had commenced as a quest for purpose had blossomed into a movement that transcended borders, uniting people under a common banner of change. He marveled at how the dance of destiny had guided him to this moment, recognizing that it was a dance that would continue indefinitely—a dance of growth, of exploration, and of transformation.

Reflecting upon his life's trajectory, Arjun understood that destiny wasn't a destination etched in stone; rather, it was a rhythmic dance, an ever-evolving choreography of possibilities. Destiny invited him to step forward with intention, infusing each movement with the authenticity of his values and the symphony of his passions. It was a dance that beckoned him to partner with the universe itself, orchestrating each step with grace and purpose.

In the dance of destiny, Arjun found his purpose, his passion, and his true self. The threads of his ancestry, the tales of his travels, and the experiences that had shaped him all converged into a harmonious melody, guiding him along a path of impact and transformation. As the world watched in awe, the ordinary had truly become extraordinary.

And so, with each sunrise and each sunset, Arjun continued to dance—a dancer, a changemaker, a thread in the grand tapestry of destiny. As his steps intertwined with the steps of countless others, a symphony of change reverberated across time and space. Destiny was no longer an enigma; it was a dance, and Arjun had learned to dance it with all the fervor of his heart and the depth of his soul.

Provocations

In the face of skepticism, Arjun remained steadfast, knowing that the virtual realm could amplify impact rather than diminish it. To address concerns, he initiated dialogue sessions, fostering transparent communication with critics and skeptics. These conversations became a platform for mutual understanding, where Arjun elucidated the network's commitment to complementing, not overshadowing, local efforts.

Arjun's response to challenges embodied the essence of a changemaker – turning adversity into opportunity. He embraced criticism as constructive feedback, refining the network's strategies and reinforcing its commitment to fostering both local and global change. His resilience became a beacon, guiding the network through turbulent waters.

Amidst these challenges, Arjun found solace in the stories of changemakers within the network. Their unwavering dedication, coupled with tangible results, provided a testament to the efficacy of virtual collaboration. These stories became powerful narratives that countered skepticism and showcased the network's tangible impact on diverse communities.

As Arjun continued to navigate the complex landscape of social impact, he remained guided by the belief that true change required adaptability, resilience, and an unwavering commitment to the values that fueled the Global Changemakers Network. Each challenge became an opportunity to refine and strengthen the network's foundations, ensuring that the dance of destiny unfolded with purpose and impact.

Arjun's introduction of "Global Changemaker Chapters" showcased his commitment to inclusivity and adaptability. By creating localized hubs, he addressed the concerns about global initiatives overshadowing local efforts, fostering a harmonious blend of both. The chapters became dynamic spaces where the tapestry of change was woven with threads of regional nuance and diversity.

These chapters not only strengthened the network's impact but also became incubators for innovative solutions tailored to specific challenges faced by different communities. Arjun's approach exemplified the transformative power of listening to feedback and responding with strategic adjustments. The network evolved into a mosaic of interconnected chapters, each contributing to the symphony of global change in its own unique way.

As the chapters flourished, so did the sense of belonging within the network. Changemakers found a space where their stories and struggles were understood on a local level yet resonated globally. The Global Changemaker Network, now more resilient and responsive, continued to demonstrate that the dance of destiny wasn't about imposing a single rhythm but embracing the diverse beats of positive change worldwide.

Arjun's commitment to his role as a changemaker came at a cost, a personal sacrifice that transcended the glamorous façade of international conferences and speaking engagements. The expansion of his network meant a constant dance with the hands of time, pulling him away from the warmth of his family and the embrace of his loved ones.

Amid the solitude imposed by his journey, Arjun sought refuge in the sanctuary of his spiritual practice. Deeply rooted in ancient wisdom, he found solace and strength within the quiet corners of meditation and the flowing movements of yoga. It was in these sacred moments that he nurtured a centered mind, an anchor in the unpredictable sea of social impact.

His spiritual connection was not a mere ritual but a lifeline, connecting him to the teachings of his ancestors and the profound wisdom handed down by his grandmother. In the gentle whispers of tradition, he discovered a compass, guiding him with love and compassion through the uncharted territories of his mission.

It was within the sacred space of meditation that Arjun unearthed a revelation that resonated with the very core of his being. Resilience, he realized, was not merely the endurance of storms but the embrace of the profound lessons they carried. Every challenge, every setback, became a sacred opportunity for growth and evolution.

In the silence, he found not only solace but also a reservoir of clarity and purpose. His journey was no longer a series of events but a tapestry woven with the threads of self-discovery and enlightenment. As he navigated the tumultuous waters of social impact, he did so with a heart open to growth and a spirit resilient in the face of adversity.

Arjun's journey with newfound wisdom propelled him to lead the Global Changemakers Network with a spirit of curiosity and an unyielding belief in the potency of collective action. Challenges were no longer obstacles but rather invitations for exploration, and setbacks were reframed as indispensable stepping stones. Arjun became a beacon of encouragement, urging changemakers to view adversities as opportunities and celebrating their triumphs with genuine joy and pride.

A pinnacle moment for the network arrived when the United Nations acknowledged its outstanding contribution to the Sustainable Development Goals. Arjun, now a recognized voice in the global arena, stood before the UN General Assembly, weaving narratives of changemakers from every corner of the world. The spotlight cast on the network's initiatives ushered in a tide of support and interest, propelling its growth and amplifying its impact.

In the midst of accolades and acclaim, Arjun remained steadfastly humble and grounded. He understood that the path of a changemaker was perpetual, an unending odyssey with endless possibilities. Arjun's innovation knew no bounds as he delved into uncharted territories, exploring novel avenues for positive change. Leveraging emerging technologies and forging strategic partnerships, he sought to magnify the network's influence on a global scale.

His interactions with changemakers bore witness to countless displays of courage, compassion, and unyielding perseverance. Ordinary individuals, confronted by extraordinary challenges, emerged as catalysts for transformation within their communities, inspiring others to join the movement.

Among these narratives, one story resonated deeply with Arjun. It was the tale of Radha, a young girl from a rural village in India. Armed with determination, Radha singlehandedly initiated a campaign to provide clean drinking water to her community. A modest contribution from her personal savings enabled the installation of a water purification system, transforming the lives of hundreds of families. Radha's story became emblematic of the profound impact an individual, fueled by passion and resilience, could have on the world.

Arjun's decision to invite Radha to share her story at the Global Changemakers Summit proved to be a transformative moment. Radha's humility and unwavering determination captivated the audience, and her simple act of kindness sent ripples of inspiration through the hearts of those in attendance. Her narrative became a catalyst, prompting others to recognize the power within themselves to effect change in their own communities.

In the quiet moments of reflection that followed, Arjun came to a profound realization. The dance of destiny wasn't merely about his personal journey; it was about empowering others to discover and embrace their unique rhythm of resilience. Each changemaker, he understood, was a vital thread woven into the tapestry of positive change, contributing to a collective symphony of impact.

The journey of Arjun and the Global Changemakers Network unfolded with each step guided by the harmonious rhythm of resilience. Challenges were met with determination and adaptability, and victories were celebrated with humility and gratitude. The tapestry they were weaving reflected not just individual stories but a shared vision of a better world.

Arjun recognized that the dance of destiny was not a solo performance; it was an ensemble featuring changemakers united by a common purpose. As they moved to the rhythm of resilience, they co-created a symphony of hope, compassion, and transformation that transcended the boundaries of time and space. In this symphony, the ordinary metamorphosed into the extraordinary.

His contemplations on interconnectedness extended beyond immediate circles. Arjun often found himself pondering the serendipitous encounter with Aisha, the young changemaker who had set him on this transformative path. He marveled at the intertwining of their stories in the grand tapestry of change, wondering about the lasting impact of their meeting and the echoes it sent through the interconnected web of lives and destinies.

As Arjun savored the evening tranquility in his garden, the gentle hum of nature accompanied by the aromatic fragrance of tea, his phone stirred to life with a message from Aisha. "Hey, Arjun. I hope you're doing well. Remember the first time we met at that bookstore?"

A nostalgic smile traced Arjun's lips as he typed, "Of course, Aisha. That meeting changed the course of my life. How have you been?"

Aisha's reply carried the vibrancy of her spirit, "I've been great! Our organization just reached a major milestone - we've impacted the lives of over a thousand children through our educational initiatives."

Pride swelled within Arjun as he read Aisha's words. "That's incredible, Aisha! Your dedication is truly inspiring. You've created a ripple effect of change."

Their conversation unfolded like a tapestry, woven with threads of shared experiences and intertwined destinies. Aisha painted vivid portraits of the children whose lives had undergone profound transformations through her organization's initiatives. She spoke of challenges met head-on and victories celebrated with unbridled joy, each story underscoring the indomitable spirit of resilience that permeated every narrative.

In those moments, Arjun realized the enduring impact of chance encounters and the interconnectedness of their stories. Aisha's journey, a parallel symphony of change, echoed the same melody of hope and transformation that resonated within the Global Changemakers Network. The threads of their lives, once casually woven together in the aisles of a bookstore, had evolved into a rich tapestry of collective change, proving that the dance of destiny was a harmonious composition played out by individuals connected by a shared vision of making the world a better place.

In the ebb and flow of their conversation, Arjun discerned a profound truth: their stories were not isolated narratives but interconnected threads contributing to the larger tapestry of positive change. Aisha's endeavors had touched the lives of those she served, and in return, her journey had ignited the spark within Arjun, propelling him onto his path of change-making.

"Arjun," Aisha typed, "do you remember the elderly woman I told you about? The one who taught me the power of storytelling?"

In the corridors of memory, Arjun revisited that conversation from years ago. "Yes, I remember. Her wisdom left a deep impression on you."

Aisha's response carried a subtle undercurrent of nostalgia. "I recently visited her again, and she's still as spirited as ever. She asked about you and how your journey was unfolding."

Touched by the enduring connection, Arjun replied, "Please tell her that her words continue to guide me. Her wisdom echoes in the work I do."

As their dialogue continued, gratitude flowed freely in their words. Both Arjun and Aisha acknowledged the threads that had intricately woven their stories together. With each shared reflection, they recognized that the dance of destiny was not confined to individual tales of impact; it was a harmonious symphony of connections linking changemakers across the vast expanse of time and space.

As their conversation drew to a close, Arjun carried with him the profound awareness that their stories, like myriad melodies in a symphony, resonated far beyond the confines of their individual journeys. The dance of destiny, he realized, was a collective masterpiece, and each connection forged along the way added depth and richness to the ever-evolving composition of positive change.

In the ensuing weeks, Arjun's contemplations reached even greater depths. He discerned that the dance of destiny was a reciprocal choreography—the impact he wove into the lives of others mirrored back in the intricate steps of his own journey. Each dialogue, every shared story, and each connection made added layers of richness to the evolving fabric of change.

One serene night, under a canvas of stars, Arjun whispered a silent gratitude to the universe. Grateful for chance encounters, for challenges met and overcome, and for the illuminating moments of epiphany that had guided his path. He acknowledged the threads of resilience, durable yet delicate, that had carried him through the undulating highs and lows of his transformative journey.

As he gazed at the night sky, Arjun felt an unspoken connection to all those who had danced the dance of destiny before him. Changemakers who had woven threads of compassion, justice, and hope into the very fabric of humanity. Their legacy lived on in the stories he shared, the initiatives he led, and the impact he crafted.

The dance of destiny, he realized, was an eternal rhythm, transcending the boundaries of individual lives and merging seamlessly into the universal symphony of change. Arjun's heart swelled with a profound sense of purpose and unity, for he understood that the ordinary had indeed become extraordinary. His journey, he recognized, was but a note in the harmonious composition of a world continually aspiring to be better.

The Symphony of Impact

Arjun's journey as a changemaker had transcended the individual notes of impact, evolving into a symphony—a collaborative masterpiece of individuals and ideas that echoed far beyond the confines of time and space. The Global Changemakers Network had burgeoned into a vibrant tapestry woven together by the shared commitment of diverse changemakers, all devoted to creating positive change.

Amid the flourishing network, Arjun found himself reflecting on the moments of connection and collaboration that defined their collective journey. One such reflection often led him back to the transformative dialogue with Aisha, a dear friend and fellow traveler on the path of change-making.

One sunlit afternoon, as Arjun ambled through a local park, his phone rang—it was Aisha. "Arjun, I just wanted to share some exciting news with you," she exclaimed.

Intrigued, Arjun responded, "Tell me, Aisha. What's the news?"

Aisha's voice radiated enthusiasm, "Our organization just received a grant to expand our initiatives to a neighboring country. Can you believe it? Our impact is spreading."

Arjun's heart swelled with joy for Aisha's success. "That's incredible, Aisha! Your dedication is truly paying off. Your journey is an inspiration to us all."

Their conversation seamlessly transitioned to reminiscing about their initial meeting at the bookstore. Aisha chuckled, "You know, Arjun, I almost didn't come to that bookstore that day. But something told me I had to be there."

As they shared laughter and memories, Arjun marveled at the serendipity that had brought them together. It was a testament to the interconnected threads of destiny, weaving together the stories of changemakers in ways that surpassed rational explanation. At that moment, amidst the sunlight dappling through the leaves, Arjun felt a profound sense of gratitude for the unpredictable beauty of their shared journey and the symphony of impact resonating across borders and boundaries.

Arjun's smile reflected the depth of gratitude for that serendipitous encounter. "And I'm so glad you did. Our meeting set off a chain of events that has transformed countless lives."

In the ebb and flow of their conversation, Arjun recognized that their stories were not isolated chapters but intricately woven threads in the grand tapestry of the network's journey. Their chance encounter had acted as a catalyst, propelling them both onto a shared path of purpose and impact.

The Impact Accelerator Program had become a crescendo in the symphony of impact. Arjun vividly recalled the day he stood before the participants at the program's summit. The hall pulsed with energy and passion as young changemakers representing diverse corners of the world fervently shared their dreams and initiatives.

During a break, Arjun engaged in conversation with Rahul, a participant who had developed an innovative solution for water conservation in urban areas. Rahul spoke animatedly about his project and the hurdles he had surmounted.

Arjun, nodding in understanding, remarked, "It's amazing what you've accomplished, Rahul. You're making a real difference."

Rahul's eyes sparkled with gratitude. "Thank you, Arjun. Your story inspired me to believe that even one person's efforts can create meaningful change."

Arjun's heart swelled with a profound sense of interconnectedness. "And your story, Rahul, is now inspiring others. That's the beauty of our network—we learn from each other and amplify our impact." As they shared these reflections, Arjun marveled at the ever-expanding ripple effect of inspiration and change, affirming that within the network's tapestry, each thread played a crucial role in the collective symphony of positive transformation

The "Symphony of Impact" ceremony at the program's summit had etched itself into the core of Arjun's being. He vividly recalled the diverse voices and stories that had converged in a harmonious composition of change, each note resonating with the spirit of unity and collaboration that defined the network.

Yet, the journey of a changemaker was not immune to challenges. Arjun's contemplations led him to a memory of a difficult decision, a crossroads where the network's values faced a stern test. The controversy surrounding a partnership had placed his commitment to integrity in the spotlight.

One evening, seated in his study and lost in thought, Arjun's wife, Maya, entered the room. Observing his furrowed brow, she inquired, "Is something bothering you, Arjun?"

Sighing, Arjun reflected the weight of his thoughts in his eyes. "Yes, Maya. We're facing a tough situation with a partner organization. Some members are questioning their ethics, and I'm torn between upholding our values and considering the potential benefits."

Maya, wise and supportive, sat beside him, offering her perspective. "Arjun, remember why you started this journey—to create positive change with integrity. I believe you'll make the right decision."

Her words struck a chord within Arjun. "You're right, Maya. Our values define us, and I can't compromise on them. It's a tough choice, but it's the only choice."

With Maya's steadfast support, Arjun navigated the challenge with transparency and inclusivity. The network's commitment to integrity remained unwavering, and the experience fortified his belief in the power of collective decision-making.

As the Global Changemakers Network commemorated its tenth year, Arjun stood in awe of the remarkable journey they had undertaken. The "Decade of Impact" celebration served as a poignant testament to the network's evolution—from a humble idea to a global movement of change. The threads of resilience, unity, and unwavering commitment to values had woven a tapestry that narrated not only a story of a decade but an enduring saga of positive transformation.

Arjun's speech at the celebration was a poignant blend of gratitude and hope, a testament to the collective journey of the changemakers. Standing before the gathering, he spoke with a voice that carried the weight of experience, weaving tales of resilience and transformation.

"Friends," Arjun began, "our journey is a dance of resilience, guided by the rhythm of impact. We've come so far, yet the path ahead is still filled with possibilities. The world needs us more than ever, and together, we can create waves of change that extend far beyond our lifetimes."

The audience, drawn into the narrative, listened with rapt attention. Arjun concluded his speech with a stirring call to action, urging everyone to continue dancing to the rhythm of resilience and to recognize the profound power of their actions, no matter how small.

As the celebration reached its conclusion, Arjun basked in a deep sense of fulfillment. The Global Changemakers Network had surpassed his wildest dreams, evolving into a beacon of hope and inspiration for individuals across the globe. The symphony of impact they had collectively orchestrated stood as a testament to the extraordinary potential within ordinary individuals to effect profound change.

And so, the journey continued—a dance of resilience, collaboration, and transformation echoing through the corridors of time. In the face of new challenges and opportunities, Arjun and the changemakers of the network remained united, steadfastly committed to turning the ordinary into the extraordinary. Together, they crafted a symphony of impact that resonated not just in the present but promised to reverberate for generations to come.

Arjun's contemplation of the Global Changemakers Network's journey led him to a profound realization – their impact transcended mere statistics. It was about the narratives, the connections forged, and the lives profoundly altered.

On a quiet evening, Arjun found himself in his study, enveloped by the memories encapsulated in photographs and mementos from the network's odyssey. Each image portrayed a moment of inspiration, a glimmer of hope, or a triumph over adversity.

His gaze settled on a photograph of Radha, the young girl hailing from a rural village in India who had brought clean drinking water to her community. Arjun vividly recalled the day he encountered Radha and how her unwavering determination had etched an indelible mark on his soul.

With a tender smile, Arjun reached for his phone and dialed Radha's number. After a few rings, Radha's voice resonated through the line.

"Hello?"

"Radha, it's Arjun," he greeted warmly. "I was reflecting on our journey and wanted to hear about how everything's unfolding on your end."

Radha's voice carried a blend of excitement and humility. "Arjun, things are progressing well. The water purification system has made a tremendous difference in our village. Children aren't falling ill as frequently, and parents are profoundly grateful."

Arjun's heart swelled with pride. "You've achieved something truly extraordinary, Radha. Your unwavering determination serves as a beacon of inspiration for us all."

Radha chuckled, her spirit radiating through the phone. "I'm just doing what needs to be done, Arjun.

I learned from you that even one person's actions can create a ripple effect."

As their conversation unfolded, Arjun recognized that Radha's story embodied the profound impact of ordinary individuals undertaking extraordinary actions. Her journey had not only transformed her village but had also ignited a spark in others, motivating them to contribute to positive change.

In the quiet of his study, surrounded by the echoes of these stories, Arjun found renewed purpose. It wasn't merely about the grand scale of their initiatives but the profound influence these tales held – each a testament to the boundless potential within every individual to be a catalyst for change.

Arjun's mind journeyed back to a vivid memory— one that had etched itself into the tapestry of his transformative experiences. It was a day when he stepped into the heart of a Global Changemaker Chapter nestled in the vibrant embrace of a bustling city. The room pulsated with an infectious energy, a synergy of diverse minds converging for a singular purpose.

During a pause in the discussions, Arjun found himself immersed in a conversation with two dynamic entrepreneurs, Malik and Sofia. Their collaboration sought to harness the prowess of technology to bridge the gaping healthcare divide in underserved communities.

In the midst of animated discourse, Malik's eyes sparkled with enthusiasm. "Arjun, we're in the throes of creating an app that will revolutionize healthcare in remote areas. Imagine connecting patients to doctors remotely."

Sofia, her voice echoing determination, added, "And we're ensuring it's user-friendly, accessible even for those with limited tech skills."

Arjun, an avid listener, absorbed the essence of their initiative. "Your project holds the promise of a profound impact. It's a harmonious fusion of innovation and empathy."

A subtle exchange of glances passed between Malik and Sofia, reflecting the depth of their commitment. "Being part of this network has been transformative for us. It's more than collaboration; it's akin to having a global family," Malik expressed, a grin playing on his lips.

In that moment, Arjun glimpsed the interconnectedness of these changemakers and the palpable sense of purpose that bound them. Their dedication resonated with him, reaffirming his belief in the mission of the network. This encounter with visionaries like Radha, Malik, and Sofia wasn't just about projects—it was a testament to the profound impact that collective action could wield. Their stories illuminated the latent potential within each individual, emphasizing the transformative power that lay dormant, waiting to be unleashed.

As Arjun continued to traverse the corridors of his memories, he marveled at the mosaic of narratives that had shaped his journey. The Global Changemaker network was more than a confluence of ideas; it was a crucible of change, igniting the dormant embers within individuals and fanning them into flames of purpose. In each interaction, in every story, Arjun found echoes of his own quest for meaning—a journey fueled by the belief that within every soul lay the capacity to instigate profound, meaningful change.

The odyssey with the Global Changemakers Network had etched into Arjun's consciousness the importance of adaptability and the embrace of new ideas. A poignant recollection surfaced—one of a conversation with Maya, a discourse that mirrored the evolving landscape of social impact.

"Arjun," Maya had asserted, her gaze penetrating the future, "the world is in a constant state of flux. New challenges surface, demanding an evolution in our approach."

Arjun, acknowledging the profound truth in her words, responded, "You're absolutely right, Maya. Our journey is a testament to the need for adaptability. It's about crafting innovative solutions that not only meet the needs of today but also anticipate the challenges of tomorrow."

As Arjun delved deeper into the corridors of retrospection, he realized that the symphony of impact they orchestrated wasn't confined to a singular melody. It was a rich composition, a tapestry woven with diverse notes—each note embodying a distinct initiative, a unique story, a voice that refused to be silenced.

Amidst his contemplations, an email from Aisha arrived, bearing a video from their transformative past. It captured a conversation at the bookstore, a moment that had set the trajectory for both their journeys.

As the video unfolded before him, Arjun was captivated by the sheer simplicity of that pivotal moment. Two souls, driven by a shared aspiration for change, had connected in a way that would not only define their destinies but also resonate in the lives of countless others.

Without hesitation, Arjun forwarded the video to Maya, accompanied by a note that bore the weight of reflection, "Look at how it all began. Every journey commences with a single step and a conversation. Our impact, Maya, is an accumulation of these seemingly small yet profoundly powerful moments."

Maya, in response, affirmed the sentiment, "Indeed, Arjun. Each conversation, each connection, possesses the latent potential to trigger a chain reaction of positive change. Your journey has been a testament to nurturing these connections and amplifying their impact on the broader canvas of societal transformation."

As the night enveloped the world in its quiet embrace, Arjun stood by the window, drawn to the celestial canvas of stars. The symphony of impact he had become a part of unfolded before him—a vast and intricate composition resonating with the beauty of harmonious collaboration. At this moment, gratitude welled within him, a profound acknowledgment of the privilege to dance to the rhythm of resilience within a network dedicated to shaping a better world, one deliberate step at a time.

Arjun's journey had been an immersive experience, a journey that exposed him to the transformative power of collaboration. He recalled a poignant conversation with Lucas, a fellow changemaker committed to environmental conservation, shared over a cup of coffee.

Lucas, with a gaze as steady as the purpose he championed, had imparted his wisdom. "Arjun, the beauty of collaboration lies in its ability to multiply our impact. When we join forces, our efforts become a force to be reckoned with, capable of surmounting even the most complex challenges."

Arjun, resonating with Lucas's insight, had nodded in agreement. "You're absolutely right. Collaboration enables us to bring diverse strengths and perspectives to the table, creating a tapestry of solutions woven with resilience and innovation."

The collaborative spirit within the network extended beyond individuals to include partnerships with corporations that echoed their shared values. Arjun reminisced about a conversation with Rhea, a corporate leader whose alliance with the network was dedicated to supporting education initiatives.

In a dialogue that transcended the traditional boundaries between social impact and business, Rhea articulated, "Arjun, social impact isn't the exclusive domain of NGOs. Businesses have a significant role to play. By converging resources and expertise, we have the potential to drive meaningful change."

Arjun, recognizing the symbiotic potential of such alliances, had acknowledged, "You're shedding light on the transformative nature of cross-sector partnerships. Together, we possess the ability to craft holistic solutions that address the multifaceted challenges woven into the fabric of society."

Among the network's myriad collaborations, one of the most impactful unions had blossomed with a technology company that shared an unwavering commitment to education and innovation. This alliance bore the fruit of a virtual learning platform, a beacon of knowledge illuminating the paths of underserved communities across the globe.

Arjun's reflections carried him back to the momentous launch of this transformative platform, a memory tinged with excitement and anticipation. In a room pulsating with the shared heartbeat of changemakers, Arjun stood, a torchbearer of their collective vision.

"We stand firm in the belief that education is a fundamental right, and technology can be the bridge that spans gaps and dismantles barriers," Arjun declared with unwavering conviction. "This platform stands as a testament to our shared dedication—a dedication to making quality education not just a privilege, but an accessible reality for all."

As the virtual learning platform gained momentum, Arjun found himself touched by a poignant message from a teacher in a remote village. The words carried the weight of transformation, "This platform has metamorphosed our classroom. Our students are now tethered to a world of knowledge, and their enthusiasm for learning is nothing short of contagious."

Those heartfelt words etched an indelible mark on Arjun's soul, tears welling in his eyes. The realization struck him with a profound force—their endeavors weren't confined to the realm of projects; they were about forging connections that touched lives, kindled dreams, and empowered individuals to ascend to their full potential.

The symphony of impact, Arjun realized, transcended the mere act of creating change. It was about cultivating a culture of empathy and understanding, a sentiment encapsulated in a powerful conversation he once had with Mateo, a fellow changemaker dedicated to fostering intercultural dialogue.

Mateo's words lingered in Arjun's reflections like a profound melody. "Change isn't just external," Mateo had shared, his insight echoing through the corridors of purpose. "It's about changing perceptions, breaking down walls, and fostering a sense of global citizenship."

Arjun, resonating with Mateo's wisdom, nodded in agreement. "You're getting to the heart of the matter. By promoting dialogue and understanding, we lay the foundation for a more inclusive and harmonious world."

The transformative power of empathy was further illuminated during the network's "Empathy Week," a global campaign designed to inspire individuals to step into someone else's shoes and embrace their experiences. A conversation with Amina, a participant in this poignant campaign, stood out in Arjun's memory.

Amina shared her perspective, "Arjun, empathy is a bridge that connects us, irrespective of our differences. When we immerse ourselves in another person's reality, we discover that our similarities far outweigh our differences."

Arjun, touched by Amina's profound understanding, responded, "You've encapsulated the very essence of our mission, Amina. Empathy is the thread that binds our global community together."

As Arjun's reflections wove through the tapestry of impact, he recognized that the symphony extended far beyond the network's initiatives—it reached into the lives of every individual touched by their work. The journey of a changemaker, he realized, was a journey of personal transformation, where ordinary individuals discovered the extraordinary potential within.

Arjun's narrative had also been about kindling the spark of resilience in the next generation of changemakers. A vivid memory surfaced—a conversation with a group of young students during a school visit.

A curious student had asked, "Why do you do what you do?"

Arjun, locking eyes with the young minds before him, had replied, "Because I believe that each of you has the power to change the world. Your ideas, your actions—they matter." In those words, he sought to plant the seeds of possibility, nurturing the budding changemakers who would one day contribute to the symphony of impact in their own unique ways.

The students exchanged excited glances, their eyes lighting up with a spark of inspiration. Arjun continued, leaning into the intimacy of the moment, "You see, change-making is not about age; it's about your willingness to make a difference. Your small steps today can create waves of impact tomorrow."

As Arjun concluded his reflections, a profound sense of purpose and fulfillment settled within him. The journey of the Global Changemakers Network has woven a tapestry of conversations, collaborations, challenges, and triumphs. It stood as a testament to the irrefutable truth that when ordinary individuals embraced the rhythm of resilience, they could collectively compose an extraordinary symphony of change.

In the quietude of his reflections, Arjun realized that the journey wasn't just about projects and initiatives; it was about the myriad connections forged, the lives touched, and the potential unearthed. The Global Changemakers Network wasn't merely a network; it was a catalyst for personal and collective transformation. As the night held the world in its embrace, Arjun stood, gazing at the stars with a heart brimming with gratitude—for the journey, for the changemakers, and for the symphony of impact that resonated far beyond the realms of ordinary existence.

> **"**
>
> Kindness shown, care shared,
> and making a difference—the
> ripples of compassion touch
> hearts far and wide
>
> **"**

6

The Whispers of Wanderlust

December 21, 2021

A Call to Adventure

As the sun dipped below the horizon, casting warm hues across the Mumbai sky, Arjun sought refuge in a hidden haven—a small park seemingly untouched by the urban tumult. Amid the ceaseless rhythm of the city, here, nature's whispers persisted amidst the symphony of life.

Seated on a weathered bench, Arjun closed his eyes, allowing the world's cacophony to recede into the background. In the tranquil cocoon of stillness, memories surfaced like fragments of a half-forgotten melody. Kasar, the village nestled amid rolling hills, echoed in his heart.

Childhood in Kasar had been a canvas painted with simplicity and joy. Amidst verdant hills and fertile fields, Arjun had been a wild sprite, chasing dreams, climbing trees, and embracing the laughter of fellow village children. The elderly spun tales of ancient heroes and mythical legends—stories that ignited his young imagination, planting seeds of curiosity and wanderlust.

Yet, as life's seasons unfolded, the dreams of youth often yielded to the pragmatic demands of adulthood. Arjun pursued education, transplanted himself to the city for career opportunities, and soared in the corporate realm. But the whispers of wanderlust, born in his childhood, persisted—a constant reminder of the yearning for purpose and a deeper connection.

In a serendipitous moment, Arjun's path intersected with an old travel journal tucked away in his attic's embrace. The journal belonged to his late father, a kindred spirit who had traversed the globe, unraveling its stories. Turning its pages, Arjun felt an inexplicable connection to his father's words. He realized that the flames of adventure and exploration, like ancestral torches, had been passed down through generations.

As the tapestry of memory unfolded, Arjun sensed a beckoning—a call to rediscover the echoes of his own dreams, to embark on a journey that transcended the boundaries of routine and expectation. The park, with its serenity and the fading glow of the Mumbai sunset, became a threshold, a space where the past intertwined with the present and the whispers of wanderlust entwined with the call of the unknown future.

The tales within the journal had breathed life into Arjun's dormant spirit—a spark that rekindled the embers of wanderlust. It was time to answer the call of the unknown, to embark on a personal voyage. With determination as his compass and a mind receptive to the unfamiliar, Arjun's first solo expedition took form. The destination beckoning him: Ladakh, a realm cradled in the Himalayas, promising rugged landscapes, ancient monasteries, and souls steeped in stories.

The flight to Leh, the capital of Ladakh, was a whirlwind of emotions. Excitement intertwined with apprehension, marking Arjun's inaugural solo odyssey—an escape from the cocoon of familiarity, a surrender to the cloak of uncertainty. As the wheels gently met the runway, Leh's crisp air enveloped him—a reminder that stepping beyond comfort zones marked the threshold to transformation.

Leh's beauty, stark and enchanting, unveiled itself before Arjun like an ancient manuscript revealing its secrets. Snow-draped peaks brushed against cerulean skies, and the grandeur of nature humbled him—a whisper of his own insignificance within the universe's vast tapestry. His days unfolded as an exploration of winding roads leading to ancient monasteries perched on rocky perches, hikes through terrains echoing with ancient stories, and the camaraderie of fellow adventurers, each with their unique journey etched on their souls.

One evening, beneath the warm embrace of a Ladakhi sunset, Arjun found himself in the company of a venerable monk at Thiksey Monastery. Their conversation wove a symphony of wisdom—a discourse on the alchemy of travel shaping perceptions and nurturing inner peace. The monk's words resonated within Arjun—an intricate melody of wanderlust interwoven with introspection, a harmonious blend that echoed through the majestic landscapes of Ladakh.

As the monk spoke, Arjun felt a resonance—a chord struck deep within him. The journey, he realized, transcended mere physical destinations; it was a quest to unearth the hidden gems within—facing fears, embracing vulnerabilities, and weaving his story into the narrative of the world.

With each passing day, Ladakh's magic deepened its grip. The village of Lamayuru, christened the "Moonland of Ladakh," became a sanctuary of reflection. Here, Arjun encountered Tashi, a young shepherd whose spirit resonated with the hills he called home. Tashi's dreams were humble—rooted in his family's well-being, his community's happiness, and the preservation of his culture.

As Arjun spent time with Tashi and his family, he marveled at their contentment amidst simplicity. In a life where yaks and goats were companions and rugged terrains a canvas, Tashi found happiness. Amidst the moon-like landscape, Arjun discovered that the pursuit of material gains often left an emptiness that the simplicity of human connections could fill.

Ladakh's embrace became a cocoon of transformation—a chrysalis where Arjun's metamorphosis unfolded. His return to Mumbai was a homecoming tinged with the fragrance of self-discovery. The whispers of wanderlust had led him not just to new horizons but to the compass of his own soul.

The echoes of Ladakh and its lessons lingered like constellations in his mind's sky, guiding his steps. The symphony of the ordinary, adorned with extraordinary significance, became a melody he now embraced—a tune that resonated with his heart's rhythm.

In the bustling heart of Mumbai, Arjun found himself navigating through the city's labyrinthine streets—not as a stranger lost in the crowd, but as a voyager who had found his inner compass. The once-hidden gems within him now sparkled with newfound radiance, and the city's pulse harmonized with the rhythm of his awakened soul.

Arjun comprehended that his journey was a mosaic—a kaleidoscope of experiences, encounters, and introspections. It was a dance with the unknown, guided not only by the pull of far-off lands but also by the yearning for self-discovery. His wanderlust transcended the mere collection of passport stamps; it was about the stories etched into the fabric of his soul.

The world, he realized, stretched out like an expansive canvas, awaiting the strokes of his experiences. The Himalayan vistas had revealed a world beyond walls—a place where mountains conversed with clouds, where the whispers of monks carried ancient wisdom, and where the laughter of young shepherds echoed across valleys.

The journal that once belonged to his father had been a portal to the past, but now it served as a compass for the future. The inked narratives had transformed into whispers of inspiration—reminders that wanderlust was a timeless melody passed from one generation to another, each verse unique yet connected.

With every step, Arjun sensed himself shedding layers accumulated over the years—the corporate armor, the city's haste, and the veneer of expectations. He embraced vulnerability, standing on the precipice of the unknown with arms wide open. The uncertainties were no longer daunting but an invitation to dance with life.

Returning to the rhythm of Mumbai, he realized that wanderlust was a mindset—a way of perceiving the world through the eyes of a traveler, even in the midst of routine. The honking streets became a symphony of diverse stories, towering buildings transformed into modern-day marvels, and every corner held the promise of discovery. In this mindset, Arjun found a perpetual adventure, a journey that extended far beyond physical landscapes into the realms of perception and appreciation.

Wanderlust wasn't confined to distant shores; it was a transformative lens that turned the familiar into the extraordinary. Arjun delved into the alleys and corners of the city, seeking beauty hidden in plain sight. He reveled in street food as if savoring exotic cuisines, explored markets as if traversing bazaars of far-off lands, and connected with strangers as if forging friendships with fellow adventurers.

Each day became an exploration—a quest to infuse life with the essence of his journeys. Arjun's travels had nurtured not only his longing for the world but also cultivated a mindset of presence—a reminder to savor each moment, whether on snow-capped mountains or amidst the urban hum.

Ladakh's landscapes had taught him that the world's beauty was a mirror reflecting the beauty within. Tashi's simplicity had revealed that joy wasn't tied to possessions but to connections and purpose. The monk's wisdom had emphasized that every step was a step towards self-realization, an odyssey of understanding the threads that wove him into the fabric of existence.

Standing at the crossroads of his journey, the whispers of wanderlust were no longer fleeting breezes—they were the very air he breathed. They had become his muse, the driving force behind his exploration of both the world and himself. The journal he had discovered wasn't just a relic; it was a torch passed on—a beacon to kindle the flames of adventure in the hearts of future wanderers.

The world awaited, its chapters untold, and Arjun was poised to script them with every footfall, every conversation, and every heartbeat. The adventure wasn't confined to distant horizons; it was alive within him, waiting to be unfurled in every new experience, every encounter that beckoned him to dance with the universe's whispers. The symphony of his wanderlust echoed through the ordinary, turning each moment into a verse in the epic ballad of his ongoing journey.

With each step, Arjun's journey of self-discovery and wanderlust continued to unfold, casting a spell that transcended time and distance. The city of Mumbai, once a backdrop to his corporate endeavors, had transformed into a canvas for his exploration—a labyrinth of stories waiting to be uncovered.

Amid the cacophony of honking horns and bustling streets, Arjun discovered sanctuaries of stillness—a quiet park, a hidden cafe, and a patch of greenery that felt like a portal to another realm. These pockets of tranquility became his secret havens, where he could close his eyes and be transported to the mountains, the monasteries, and the moon-like landscapes of Ladakh.

His wanderlust had ignited not only a desire for external exploration but also a profound introspection. Arjun questioned the notions of success and fulfillment ingrained in him by society. He redefined his priorities, recognizing that the richness of life wasn't measured in material possessions but in moments of connection, in experiences that left imprints on the soul.

Arjun's perspective had evolved, and with it, his interactions with others deepened. Conversations became more than mere exchanges of words; they were bridges to understanding different worldviews to connecting with the human experiences that spanned continents. He found himself engaging with strangers as if they were fellow travelers sharing the same journey of life.

One evening, while sipping chai at a street stall, Arjun struck up a conversation with an elderly man named Rajan. They exchanged stories—the wanderings of a young adventurer and the life lessons of a seasoned soul. Rajan's eyes sparkled with nostalgia as he recounted his own travels, each tale a testament to the universality of human aspirations and dreams. In that shared moment, under the flickering streetlight, the symphony of their stories created a harmony that echoed through the bustling city.

"Young man," Rajan said, his voice carrying the wisdom of years, "wanderlust is the compass of the heart. It leads us to places unseen and within—reminding us that life's true treasures are the memories we create, the connections we forge, and the moments we cherish."

Arjun felt a kinship with Rajan, a connection that transcended generations. In their stories, he saw a continuum of wanderers, each adding their verses to the ever-evolving ballad of exploration. He realized that wanderlust wasn't confined to a specific age or time—it was a flame that burned eternally, passed from one seeker to another.

As Arjun's journey of wanderlust continued, he couldn't help but marvel at the interconnectedness of his experiences. The landscapes of Ladakh had mirrored the landscapes of his heart—majestic, untamed, and open to the winds of change. His encounters with monks, young shepherds, and wise elders were threads woven into the tapestry of his own evolution.

He had discovered that wanderlust wasn't just about the physical act of traveling; it was a state of mind—an openness to the world's vastness and the soul's depth. It was an invitation to step beyond the known, to embrace the unfamiliar, and to celebrate the symphony of diversity that existed within and around him.

As he stood on the shores of his own being, Arjun acknowledged that his journey of wanderlust was an ongoing saga—a tale without an end, a dance without a final curtain call. The whispers that had beckoned him to distant lands now echoed within his heart, guiding him to explore not only the external world but also the uncharted territories of his own soul.

And so, as the sun dipped below the horizon once again, casting its golden glow over the city, Arjun's heart resonated with the rhythm of wanderlust. The journal of his father, the landscapes of Ladakh, and the conversations with kindred spirits—all converged into a melody that was uniquely his own. The symphony of his wanderlust continued a song without a conclusion, an eternal dance with the universe.

With every step he took, Arjun embraced the call to adventure, dancing to the symphony of the universe's whispers. His journey was a testament to the fact that wanderlust wasn't just a desire—it was a way of being, an embodiment of curiosity, courage, and connection. As the world continued to spin its tales, Arjun was ready to script his own—a chronicle of wanderlust woven with the threads of exploration, introspection, and the magic of the unknown. The path ahead unfolded like an unwritten poem, and with each stride, he penned verses that echoed the harmonious rhythm of a life well-lived.

Embracing the Symphony Within

The melodies of Arjun's journey continued to weave their magic, intertwining with the tapestry of his soul as he embarked on a new chapter of growth. Mumbai, with its bustling streets and vibrant energy, had transformed from a backdrop to a canvas—an urban landscape where Arjun painted his symphony of transformation.

The park, once a refuge, now became a stage for Arjun's contemplation. The ancient banyan tree stood as a steadfast witness to his evolution, its branches reaching out like arms embracing his reflections. In the presence of nature's serenity, Arjun found the space to nurture the seeds of inspiration that had sprouted within him.

His Ladakh journey had marked the turning point, awakening a dormant sense of purpose and igniting his passion for exploration. The tales of his father's travel journal had bridged the gap between generations, reminding Arjun that he was part of a symphony that transcended time—an orchestra of wanderers united by the yearning for the unknown.

The virtual chronicle he had started, "The Wanderer's Symphony," became a canvas for his tales—a canvas where he painted the hues of his experiences, the shadows of his reflections, and the luminous strokes of human connection. With every story, he added his own melodies to the grand symphony of human experience.

Messages from readers echoed through the corridors of his digital sanctuary—a testament to the resonant power of storytelling. Among these voices was Riya's, a soul entangled in the web of anxiety. Arjun's words had become a lifeline, a lifeline that tugged at Riya's heartstrings and beckoned her to step out of her comfort zone. The connection forged through storytelling became a beacon of light in the vast landscape of human experience, illustrating the profound impact of sharing one's journey.

"Your words have given me the strength to believe in myself," Riya's email had read, "I've always dreamed of traveling, but fear has held me back. Your stories make me feel like I can conquer those fears."

"Riya, I was once where you are now," Arjun replied, his words carrying a gentle reassurance. "Fear is like a locked door; you hold the key. It's about taking that first step, even if it's a small one. And I'm here to help you find that key."

Their correspondence became a dialogue of transformation. As they shared their fears and dreams, Arjun realized that he was not just a storyteller; he was a mentor guiding Riya through uncharted waters. He offered the compass of his experience, helping her navigate the tides of uncertainty with courage and grace.

Arjun's blog, once a simple repository of tales, had evolved into a beacon of inspiration. His words resonated with seekers and dreamers, igniting flames of hope and introspection. His stories were like lanterns, guiding others through the labyrinth of life, reminding them that they were not alone on this symphonic journey.

Yet, Arjun's odyssey didn't stop at storytelling—it transcended into the realm of mindfulness and meditation. Like a maestro conducting an orchestra, he realized that the harmony of his life required alignment from within. Guided by his thirst for self-discovery, he delved into meditation workshops and retreats, seeking to uncover the secrets of his soul.

Meditation became his silent symphony—a dance of thoughts and emotions orchestrated by the baton of his breath. With each inhale and exhale, he explored the caverns of his mind, unraveled his fears, and embraced the stillness that resided within. The symphony of his inner world echoed in the notes of his writing, infusing his words with a newfound depth. The journey of self-discovery became a harmonious dance, intertwining with the melody of his wanderlust-infused life.

Arjun's newfound clarity had also resonated in his professional life. A renowned global consulting firm recognized his ability to orchestrate human connections and invited him to lead a project that aligned seamlessly with his passion for understanding the human experience.

The corridors of his office became an extension of his creative canvas—a space where he wove empathy and insight into every customer journey map. The brands he worked with weren't just entities; they were threads in the universal tapestry of stories waiting to be told. His projects were melodies notes of connection that played a pivotal role in customers' lives.

"Arjun, your approach is refreshing," his colleague remarked during a brainstorming session. "It's like you're composing a symphony of emotions through these customer experiences."

Arjun smiled, the metaphor resonating with his own journey. "Every interaction we design is a note in the symphony of life. Each note contributes to the melody of human connection."

As the years flowed like movements in a symphony, Arjun's blog blossomed into a platform of growth, wisdom, and connection. Workshops and online courses became vessels for seekers eager to embrace the melodies of their lives. Among these seekers was Riya, who had evolved from a reader to a fellow traveler on the path of mindfulness.

One evening, under the starlit sky of a mindfulness retreat, Arjun found himself addressing a room filled with kindred spirits. He recounted his journey, from the quiet park benches of Mumbai to the towering peaks of Ladakh to the corridors of a corporate world that had become a canvas for his creativity. As his words flowed, he saw Riya's face—a portrait of transformation—among the sea of faces before him. The room resonated with the shared melody of their collective growth and self-discovery.

"The symphony within us is a journey of transformation," he shared, his voice resonating with a profound resonance. "It's about turning fear into courage, chaos into clarity, and solitude into connection."

Riya's eyes sparkled with understanding. She had embraced the melodies within her, transforming them into a harmonious crescendo of self-awareness and growth. Her evolution was a testament to the power of the symphony that played within each of us—a symphony that Arjun had come to embrace as his guiding light.

As the retreat concluded, Arjun stood beneath the starry canopy of the night sky, his heart filled with serene contentment. He gazed at the constellations, each star a reminder of the interconnectedness of all things. Life's symphony, he realized, was composed of moments— moments of awe, moments of growth, moments of connection.

Arjun had moved from being a wanderer to a conductor, orchestrating the melodies of his life. The whispers of wanderlust, the tales of his father's travel journal, and the lessons of mindfulness had merged into a harmonious composition—a composition that resonated with the universe itself.

As he closed his eyes, he felt the rhythm of his breath synchronize with the rhythm of the universe. Each inhalation and exhalation was a note, a vibration in the grand symphony of existence. And as he stood there, surrounded by the celestial orchestra above, he knew that his journey was a perpetual symphony—an ever-evolving masterpiece of wanderlust, mindfulness, and the symphony within.

In the symphony of Arjun's life, the transformative notes resonated not only in the personal chambers of his existence but also harmonized with the very fabric of his professional journey. His metamorphosis did not unfold as a mere melody but as a complex orchestration of growth, where dissonant chords of challenges resolved into harmonious compositions of understanding and enlightenment.

Within the structured walls of the corporate world, Arjun's creativity flowed freely, weaving customer journey maps that transcended functionality to become poignant musical compositions. His designs weren't just strategic; they were symphonies of empathy and insight, orchestrating connections that could profoundly impact lives.

"Arjun, your approach is poetry for the soul," his colleague remarked during a brainstorming session. "You're transforming customer experiences into an intricate symphony."

Arjun's serene smile reflected the internal symphony he had conducted. "Just as a symphony requires various instruments to create harmony, every interaction should resonate with the chords of human connection."

Time unfolded like the movements of a grand symphony, and Arjun's blog burgeoned into a garden of wisdom and connection. His workshops and online courses became vessels for seekers, individuals yearning to uncover the melodies within their lives. Among these seekers was Riya, who evolved from a passive reader into an active participant on the mindful path.

Under the stars of a transformative mindfulness retreat, Arjun stood before an audience of kindred spirits. His narrative unfolded like a musical score, spanning from the serene corners of Mumbai to the majestic landscapes of Ladakh and the boardrooms of corporate life. Each word was a note, and each pauses a rest, creating a symphony of his life's journey. As his words wove through the air, he spotted Riya's face—a canvas of transformation—among the sea of attentive expressions, a living testament to the transformative power of the symphony he had conducted in both his life and the lives of those he touched. At that moment, under the celestial canopy, Arjun's life became a symphony, each note an invitation for others to discover the melodies within their own existence.

"Our symphony is an expedition of transformation," he shared, his voice resonating with deep introspection. "It's the art of transforming vulnerability into strength, chaos into clarity, and solitude into connection."

Riya's eyes shimmered with realization. She had not only heard the melodies within but had woven them into a symphony of self-awareness and growth. Her evolution stood as a testament to the transformative power of the symphony that resonated within each individual—a symphony that had become Arjun's guiding compass.

As the retreat drew to a close, Arjun stood beneath the starlit tapestry of the night sky, his heart brimming with tranquility. The constellations sparkled overhead, not just distant stars but manifestations of the interconnectedness of existence. Life's symphony, he realized, was woven from moments—moments of wonder, moments of transformation, moments of connection.

From a wanderer to a conductor, Arjun had orchestrated his journey's melodies. The echoes of wanderlust, the tales of his father's journal, and the teachings of mindfulness had blended into a harmonious composition—an opus resonating with the universe's rhythm.

With his eyes shut, Arjun felt his breath intertwine with the cosmic cadence. Each inhalation and exhalation harmonized with the universe's notes, forming a melody that transcended the confines of time and space. As he stood there, surrounded by the celestial symphony, he embraced the truth that his journey was an eternal symphony—a perpetually evolving masterpiece of wanderlust, mindfulness, and the symphony within.

66

Taking small steps, persevering in the journey, and inspiring others along the way lead to achieving remarkable things

99

7

Cadence of Strength

February 6, 2022

Embracing the Storm

The crucible of life had always tested the mettle of the human spirit, and Arjun's journey, a voyage into the depths of mindfulness and self-discovery, had been no stranger to trials. Through these tribulations, he uncovered a profound truth: resilience wasn't about avoiding life's tempests but embracing them as opportunities for profound growth.

On a particular day, as rain cascaded over Mumbai, transforming the bustling city into a canvas of glistening wetness, Arjun faced a storm of a different nature—a sudden and unexpected health crisis. The diagnosis crashed into his life like a bolt of lightning, illuminating the previously uncharted territories of vulnerability and uncertainty.

Lying in the hospital bed, staring at the ceiling, Arjun grappled with a torrent of emotions. The serenity he had carefully nurtured seemed to have evaporated, leaving behind an unsettled sea of apprehension. Yet, amidst this tempest, he sought refuge in the practices he had long championed—mindfulness and self-compassion. These weren't abstract concepts; they became lifeboats, navigating him through the storm.

During the seemingly endless days of recovery, Arjun found solace in an old friend—writing. His journal became a sacred space, the pages transforming into a canvas for his thoughts, fears, and reflections. His pen, like a dancer, moved gracefully across the paper, capturing the essence of his journey through resilience. Through this narrative, he deciphered the delicate choreography of strength and vulnerability—a dance that required both self-compassion and unwavering determination.

In the crucible of adversity, Arjun discovered that true resilience wasn't the absence of vulnerability but the courage to face it head-on. His journey through the storm became a testament to the transformative power of embracing life's challenges, turning them into stepping stones toward a deeper understanding of strength and the resilient spirit that resides within.

As days seamlessly melted into weeks, Arjun found himself surrounded by a symphony of compassion and empathy that formed his robust support system. Friends, family, and even the readers of his blog extended their love and encouragement, weaving a protective cocoon around him. In this intricate tapestry of care, each message, each word of support, resonated like a chord in the symphony of healing that echoed within him.

Among the visitors, one face stood out—the living embodiment of the impact of his work. Riya, the young woman whose inspiration had sprung from Arjun's words, closely followed his health updates. Her decision to be physically present became a poignant melody of hope in the midst of the storm.

Riya's visit unfolded as a soothing balm for Arjun's soul. Her vibrant spirit and the personal growth she had undergone were tangible proof of the potency of resilience. Witnessing her radiate confidence reaffirmed his belief in the transformative power of his work.

As Arjun's health gradually improved, he recognized that resilience was not a solitary pursuit but a harmonious symphony of shared strength. It was about leaning on others during moments of adversity, allowing vulnerability to stand as a testament to the depth of human connection.

In the quiet moments of convalescence, Arjun's mind sparked with an idea that would turn his personal ordeal into a force for good. He envisioned a platform that could unite individuals who, like him, had weathered their own storms and emerged stronger. Thus, "Rhythms of Resilience" was born—a virtual sanctuary where stories of triumph could inspire others to navigate their own adversities. This platform became a testament to the symphony of shared strength, echoing the belief that through collective resilience, individuals could find solace and inspiration in each other's melodies of triumph.

Arjun's call to those with stories of resilience turned into a crescendo of affirmation, a harmonious chorus of voices eager to contribute their tales of courage and determination to "Rhythms of Resilience." The platform quickly became adorned with narratives that spanned the vast spectrum of the human experience, each one a unique note in the symphony of human triumph.

Through "Rhythms of Resilience," Arjun aimed to infuse hope and strength into those navigating their own storms. The platform transformed into a digital haven, offering solace, resources, and a rich tapestry of narratives to embolden the weary. Support groups, workshops on mindfulness and self-compassion, and a global network of kindred spirits became the pillars of this virtual sanctuary.

Understanding that resilience wasn't a one-time event but an ongoing dance, Arjun emphasized the importance of continuous practice. Life's tempests, unpredictable in arrival and varied in intensity, could be navigated through mindfulness, meditation, and the embrace of vulnerability.

In the aftermath of his health crisis, Arjun's story captured the attention of wellness advocates, leading to an invitation to speak at a wellness summit. On stage, he intertwined his journey of resilience with the profound influence of mindfulness in traversing life's tumultuous seas. His words resonated deeply with the audience, and individuals approached him afterward, gratitude brimming in their eyes as they shared their own tales of resilience.

One interaction stood out among the rest—a young woman named Aisha, teetering on the edge of hopelessness. The pandemic had claimed her job, leaving her adrift. Arjun listened attentively to her story, offering words of encouragement and support. Aisha's eyes sparkled with renewed determination as Arjun's guidance reignited her passions and purpose.

In that moment, the symphony of shared strength played on, illustrating the transformative impact of resilience, empathy, and the interconnectedness of human stories.

In the subsequent weeks, Arjun became Aisha's mentor, guiding her on a transformative journey of rediscovery. Through mindfulness practices, Aisha unearthed her strengths and passions, eventually nurturing a social impact initiative that provided vocational training to marginalized youth.

As "Rhythms of Resilience" continued to ascend, Arjun felt an insatiable urge to amplify its impact. He recognized that the curated stories had the potential to touch lives beyond the digital realm. An encounter with a renowned publishing house resulted in a new project—a book titled "Rhythms of Resilience: Triumph Over Adversity." The book resonated with readers worldwide, igniting sparks of hope in hearts across the globe.

With the book's success, Arjun fortified the "Rhythms of Resilience" platform, enveloping it with more resources and support than ever before. The storm that had once threatened to drown him now propelled him toward his mission—to kindle the flames of hope, foster resilience, and uplift those navigating their own storms.

The night of the storm and the diagnosis had become poignant milestones, reminding Arjun of life's impermanence and the urgency of cherishing every moment. He realized that resilience wasn't about conquering life's challenges; it was about gracefully weathering them, viewing them as stepping stones to growth and strength.

As the melodies of "Rhythms of Resilience" echoed through the lives it touched, Arjun embraced life's cadence with renewed purpose. He understood that the storms that had once seemed insurmountable had now become the driving force behind his mission—to inspire, support, and to help others find their own rhythm of resilience. In this symphony of shared strength, Arjun's journey had transformed into a harmonious anthem of hope, echoing far beyond the confines of his personal story.

Amidst the unpredictable symphony of life, Arjun had deftly navigated through storms that raged both in his soul and in the skies. Each challenging note and every chord of adversity had become instruments, shaping him into the conductor of his own resilience. He orchestrated a harmonious blend of vulnerability and strength, transforming his journey into a dance of growth—a testament to the indomitable spirit that can rise again and again.

His path was far from linear, weaving through the unpredictable rhythms of existence. It was not just a journey but a profound odyssey, marked by February 6, 2022—a day etched into his memory like the rhythmic patter of raindrops against the window, accompanied by the gentle whispers of monsoon winds. This date heralded the beginning of another chapter in Arjun's life, one titled "Embracing the Storm," emphasizing how life's tempests could serve as catalysts for extraordinary growth.

Life's orchestration had tested Arjun's fortitude in unprecedented ways, immersing him in the realms of mindfulness and self-discovery. Armed with a new lens, resilience was no longer about avoiding adversities but about dancing with them in the storm, evolving with each step of the rhythm.

The storm that struck on that fateful day was not the tempestuous weather outside; it was an unforeseen health crisis. The diagnosis arrived like a thunderclap, shattering the tranquility Arjun had so painstakingly cultivated within himself. In the hospital bed, as he stared at the ceiling, a torrent of emotions enveloped him—fear, uncertainty, vulnerability. Yet, within this whirlwind, he reached for the tools he had spent years honing: mindfulness and self-compassion.

In the quiet sanctuary of his own mind, Arjun confronted the storm within. Instead of being overwhelmed by fear, he embraced the uncertainty. His vulnerability became a source of strength as he navigated the tempest with a newfound resilience. The hospital room transformed into a battleground where the war was fought not just with medical complexities but with the profound depths of his own being.

As Arjun faced the unknown, he discovered that the journey of self-discovery was not a tranquil pond but a vast, turbulent sea. Each wave of challenge brought the opportunity to redefine himself, and in the midst of the storm, he found a serenity that transcended the chaos. The journey became a profound lesson: that even in the face of life's fiercest storms, one could find not just survival but growth, not just resilience but transformation.

As days unfolded into weeks, Arjun sought solace in the refuge of his journal. Words cascaded from his pen like the gentle cadence of raindrops—each sentence a profound drop of introspection, each page a canvas painted with the palette of his emotions. Through the act of writing, he delved into the intricate choreography between vulnerability and strength, discovering that resilience wasn't a one-sided battle but the rhythmic dance of life.

A symphony of compassion and empathy enveloped Arjun from all corners of his existence. Friends, family, and even those who had never crossed paths with him in person orchestrated a chorus of encouragement, and each 0notes a chord in the harmony of healing. Amidst this symphony, one voice resonated with particular significance—Riya, whose life had been transformed by Arjun's journey, arrived to share in his triumph. Her presence became a melody of hope, a reminder of the profound impact one individual's resilience could have on others.

As Arjun's health improved, a realization dawned upon him: resilience wasn't a solo performance; it was a symphony. Vulnerability wasn't a sign of weakness; it was an invitation to lean on others for support. With this profound insight, an idea took root—an idea that would give rise to "Rhythms of Resilience." This platform aimed to collect and share stories of those who had weathered storms, emerging as stronger versions of themselves.

Arjun extended invitations to individuals whose narratives embodied resilience—survivors, changemakers, and ordinary individuals who had triumphed over adversity. The response was a crescendo of voices eager to share their tales. "Rhythms of Resilience" blossomed into a sanctuary of triumph, with each narrative serving as a note that resonated with hearts yearning for inspiration.

Yet, Arjun's journey remained far from linear. The resilience he spoke of wasn't a one-time achievement; it was a melody he would play again and again. Life's storms, unpredictable and unannounced, would continue to surge. However, armed with mindfulness, meditation, and a community that shared his rhythm, Arjun stood prepared to weather them all, turning each challenge into a verse in the ever-evolving symphony of his life.

Arjun's story, a digital tapestry of resilience, transcended the virtual realm. The invitation to speak at a wellness summit was a crescendo, a moment where the symphony of his journey reached new heights. On that stage, Arjun wove his narrative of resilience, seamlessly integrating the profound impact of mindfulness in navigating life's turbulent waters. As his words resonated, he witnessed familiar emotions reflected in the eyes of the audience. Post-talk, a young woman named Aisha approached—a fellow traveler through the storms of life.

Aisha's tale echoed with Arjun's own. The pandemic had thrust her into a tempest, leaving her adrift. Arjun listened intently, extending guidance and support. Aisha's eyes sparkled with hope as Arjun's words rekindled her determination. In the ensuing weeks, he served as her mentor, directing her towards rediscovering passions and finding purpose in adversity.

The thriving success of "Rhythms of Resilience" extended beyond digital boundaries. Arjun's encounter with a publishing house materialized into a book—a compilation of stories titled "Rhythms of Resilience: Triumph Over Adversity." This literary symphony resonated with readers worldwide, becoming a beacon of hope amidst life's tempests.

With the book's triumph, Arjun expanded the platform's offerings. The storm that had once threatened to break him now propelled him towards his mission—to inspire, to support, and to stand as a living testament to the power of resilience.

Arjun acknowledged that his journey was an ongoing dance, an ever-evolving symphony. Life's melodies would continue to shift, bringing both crescendos and lulls. Yet, armed with mindfulness, compassion, and a community attuned to the cadence of strength, he stood poised to rise and dance again. In composing his unique melody of resilience, Arjun not only orchestrated his life but became the conductor of a universal anthem—one that echoed with the collective strength of those who dared to dance amidst the storms.

In the grand symphony of life, Arjun's journey unfolded like a rich composition—an intricate interplay of resilience, growth, and the unwavering human spirit. The narrative of February 6, 2022, stood as a testament to this composition—a chapter eloquently titled "Embracing the Storm."

Arjun's life had been a symphony of diverse experiences, each note contributing to the melodic tapestry of his existence. As he delved deeper into the realms of mindfulness and self-discovery, he came to a profound realization: resilience was not merely a quality; it was a dance with life's challenges, a rhythm that required him to find harmony between vulnerability and strength.

The day commenced like any other, raindrops composing a gentle rhythm against his windowpane. Yet, this day marked the inception of a new movement in Arjun's symphony, a movement that would encapsulate the essence of resilience. As the rain poured outside, he found himself facing a different storm—a sudden health crisis that demanded courage and determination.

The news struck him with the force of a powerful crescendo—an unexpected chord reverberating through his being. Lying in the hospital bed, he navigated a storm of emotions—fear, uncertainty, vulnerability. However, within this turmoil, he discovered solace in the practices he had cultivated over time. Mindfulness, once a distant concept, became his refuge, guiding him through the turbulent waves of his thoughts.

During his recovery, Arjun turned to writing—a form of self-expression that had always resonated with him. With pen in hand, he poured his thoughts onto paper, each word a brushstroke on the canvas of his emotions. Through his writing, he explored the delicate balance between vulnerability and strength, realizing that resilience wasn't about erecting walls but about embracing the ebb and flow of life. The written words became the musical notes of his healing, composing a melody that echoed the harmony of his newfound understanding.

As days seamlessly transformed into weeks, Arjun became acutely aware of the profound power embedded in human connection. Messages of unwavering support cascaded in from friends, family, and even strangers whose lives had been touched by his journey. Among these voices was Riya, a young woman inspired by Arjun's writings. Her visit served as a poignant reminder of the lasting impact one individual could have on others—a humbling realization that added layers of depth to his own narrative.

With the steady improvement of his health, Arjun began to perceive resilience as a collective experience. It wasn't merely an individual endeavor but a shared journey—a dance where each partner leaned on the other during moments of vulnerability, creating a beautiful and harmonious melody of support.

From this realization sprouted the idea of "Rhythms of Resilience"—an ambitious endeavor to gather stories of triumph over adversity. Arjun extended invitations to those who had faced life's storms head-on, and the response was nothing short of overwhelming. The platform evolved into a vibrant tapestry of narratives, each thread weaving a testament to the indomitable strength of the human spirit.

Yet, the journey remained far from linear. Resilience wasn't a single note—it was a recurring melody, a continuous dance with life's tempests. Storms persisted, testing Arjun's resolve. Armed with the tools of mindfulness, meditation, and the unwavering support of his community, he found assurance that he could weather any tempest that came his way.

Invitations to speak at wellness summits and conferences followed, amplifying Arjun's message of resilience. One particular encounter left an indelible mark—an encounter with Aisha, a young woman grappling with job loss due to the pandemic. Listening to her story, Arjun recognized a familiar tune of uncertainty. Through mentorship and mindfulness, he guided Aisha to rediscover her strengths and passions, inspiring her to embark on a new journey—a testament to the transformative ripple effect of resilience.

"Rhythms of Resilience" continued its flourishing journey, surpassing the confines of the digital realm. It evolved into a symphony of hope, its harmonies resonating deeply with hearts in search of strength. Arjun's collaboration with a publishing house gave rise to "Rhythms of Resilience: Triumph Over Adversity," a transformative book that reached the lives of countless readers.

As Arjun reflected on his own odyssey, he grasped the essence of resilience—it was an ongoing dance, a cadence of strength. Life's melodies, he understood, would perpetually shift, presenting both challenges and moments of respite. Yet, armed with mindfulness, compassion, and a supportive community attuned to the rhythm of resilience, he felt prepared to dance through life's storms, composing his own unique symphony of strength.

Contemplating the stormy night that had precipitated his health crisis, Arjun recognized it as a turning point—an awakening to the transient nature of life and the imperative of cherishing each fleeting moment. For him, resilience was a melody that played on, a rhythm that would guide him through life's ever-changing tempos. In this realization, he found not just strength but a profound connection to the essence of existence—a melody of resilience that echoed through the corridors of his being, shaping the ongoing composition of his life.

Navigating the Wilderness

Arjun's journey through the symphony of resilience had become a revelation—a crescendo of growth, compassion, and the triumphant spirit of humanity. Each chapter in his life had woven a unique melody, and as time flowed like an ever-evolving composition, Arjun discovered himself navigating uncharted territories with a heart attuned to the symphonies of life.

Amidst the global workshops and speaking engagements that marked his worldly endeavors, Arjun still found solace in the wilderness that had initiated this transformative path. On a crisp morning, he stood at the edge of a dense forest, its towering trees swaying like the notes of an unsung melody. The earthy scent and the gentle rustle of leaves created a symphony of their own.

Venturing deeper into the wilderness, Arjun was enveloped by a sense of awe. The sun's golden fingers broke through the foliage, casting intricate patterns of light on the forest floor. In these serene moments, the world felt vast yet intricately connected—a reflection of the resilience that bound all living beings.

Amidst the wild tapestry, Arjun encountered a wise old man, his face etched with the marks of time and experience. Their conversation flowed like a river, winding through the valleys of life's mysteries. The old man, a guardian of ancient wisdom, shared stories of resilience passed down through generations. Each tale became a testament to the enduring strength hidden within the human soul.

"The wilderness," the old man mused, "teaches us the art of resilience. Just as trees withstand storms and seasons, so do we endure life's challenges. Nature's symphony is a constant reminder that resilience isn't just a concept—it's a song that echoes through the ages, connecting us to the enduring spirit within ourselves and the world around us."

Absorbing the ancient wisdom from the roots of the forest, Arjun nodded in silent gratitude. The old man's words echoed within him as he retraced his steps back to the city, ready to carry this newfound insight into his ongoing mission.

Back in the urban symphony, Arjun found himself approached by a group of young students who had attended his workshops. Their eyes gleamed with determination as they shared plans for a community project aimed at helping underprivileged children. Their resilience, born from personal life experiences, struck a deep chord within him.

Choosing to mentor them, Arjun guided the students through the complexities of turning their dreams into reality. The symphony of their shared purpose resonated through late-night strategy sessions, and each notes a reflection of their commitment to making a difference.

The project, now named "Harmony of Hope," began to take shape. Arjun witnessed with pride as the students rallied their community, sparking resilience in the hearts of those they touched. The symphony of their efforts echoed through every milestone—the smiles of the supported children, the sense of unity fostered, and the echoes of hope reverberating through their neighborhood.

As the project flourished, Arjun's journey once again carried him to distant lands. Standing on the edge of a cliff, overlooking a serene lake embraced by snow-capped mountains, he shared the moment with Lila, a young woman whose eyes mirrored the beauty of nature's symphony.

Lila, having overcome personal adversity, had embarked on a journey of self-discovery, embracing the wilderness both within and around her as a source of strength. Their dialogue flowed like a river, weaving tales of resilience, empowerment, and the symphony of transformation. Together, they stood on the precipice of possibility, their stories harmonizing with the vast landscape—a testament to the enduring melody of growth and resilience that echoed through the interconnected symphony of their lives.

"I've learned that every experience, no matter how challenging, adds a unique note to the symphony of our lives," Lila remarked, her voice carrying the weight of her journey.

Arjun smiled, his heart resonating with her words. "Indeed, each note shapes the melody we compose—one of growth, harmony, and the triumph of the human spirit."

Back in the heart of the city, Arjun's impact continued to evolve. The "Rhythms of Resilience" movement had surpassed his wildest dreams, echoing through lives in ways he could have never predicted. His platform had become a haven where stories converged, where shared struggles became a chorus of empowerment.

Amidst his global pursuits, Arjun received a letter that warmed his heart. It was from Aryan, the young man who had courageously shared his battles with mental health during one of Arjun's workshops. The letter spoke of Aryan's journey towards healing—a testament to the symphony of resilience that had become his anthem.

Aryan's journey had propelled him to the forefront of mental health advocacy, where his voice rang out like a clarion call for change. Through his experiences and the symphonies of others, he had discovered the transformative power of vulnerability and compassion.

With every note of Aryan's journey, Arjun's conviction deepened. The symphony of resilience was a chorus that spanned the human experience—an intricate composition that defied the boundaries of culture, age, and circumstance. As the years wove their tapestry, Arjun knew that his journey was far from over. He was a conductor in this symphony, a guardian of stories, and a guide to the resilience that lay within every heart.

One evening, as the city's lights painted the sky with myriad hues, Arjun stood once more on his rooftop sanctuary. The symphony of his own life had seamlessly harmonized with the world's melodies. In every connection, every shared story, he found echoes of his purpose—a purpose that transcended time, touching lives and kindling the flames of resilience.

As the stars began to twinkle above him, Arjun felt the symphony of resilience persist—a melody woven into the very fabric of existence. With each passing day, his mission expanded, his symphony resonating louder, echoing across generations. In the cadence of strength, he discovered not just his purpose but his legacy—an eternal symphony that would continue to empower souls long after his own notes had faded.

Arjun's journey through the symphony of resilience had become a harmonious dance with the rhythm of life itself. The world had transformed into his stage, and every experience, every encounter, added a unique note to the melody of his existence. With each step he took, he felt the symphony resonate within him, guiding him through uncharted territories of the human spirit.

On one misty morning, Arjun found himself amidst the ancient ruins of a forgotten civilization. The stones whispered stories of endurance, their silent symphony echoing through the ages. As he ran his fingers along the weathered walls, he felt a profound connection to the resilience of those who had walked this path before him.

A soft voice broke his reverie. A young woman named Zara stood beside him, her eyes mirroring the same sense of wonder. She shared tales of her own journey—the struggles she had faced, the mountains she had climbed, and the symphony of her resilience that had led her to this moment. Their dialogue became a seamless integration of stories—a symphony of shared experiences, intertwining the echoes of the past with the cadence of their present.

"Resilience," Zara mused, "it's not just about weathering storms, but about embracing the storms within us, finding strength in vulnerability."

Arjun nodded, his heart resonating with her profound insight. "Indeed, it's the sum of our experiences—the highs and lows—that composes the melody of our lives."

As Arjun's influence continued to grow, he remained steadfast in his commitment to nurturing the spark of resilience in others. He organized symposiums, creating spaces where individuals from diverse backgrounds could openly share their stories. In these gatherings, the symphony of resilience flowed freely, each narrative adding depth to the collective understanding of what it meant to overcome and thrive.

In the midst of his busy schedule, Arjun received a message from a young man named Raj. Raj had been a participant in one of Arjun's early workshops, and his journey had been a symphony of transformation. Despite numerous setbacks, Raj had emerged stronger, his spirit resonating with the chords of resilience.

Raj's message extended an invitation to his art exhibition—a celebration of his journey depicted on canvas. Arjun attended, standing amidst the vibrant colors and intricate strokes that portrayed the symphony of Raj's life. Their conversation flowed, a harmonious exchange of experiences that had shaped their paths.

"This exhibition," Raj said, "is a testament to the power of art as a medium to express and heal. Each stroke represents a note in my symphony of resilience." The gallery, filled with Raj's visual narrative, became a testament to the universal language of resilience—a language that transcended spoken words, echoing through the strokes of a paintbrush and the vibrant hues of life's canvas.

Arjun smiled, a sense of pride welling within him. "And your symphony resonates with everyone who witnesses it—a universal language of strength and triumph."

Back in the heart of the city, Arjun's own symphony continued to evolve. The "Rhythms of Resilience" movement had grown into a force that transcended borders, cultures, and languages. It became a sanctuary where souls found solace, a bridge connecting individuals from all walks of life.

One evening, Arjun was approached by an elderly man named Khaled. Khaled had been a distant observer of Arjun's journey, following his stories through the years. He spoke of his own experiences—the symphony of his life that had spanned decades, with notes of resilience woven into every chapter.

"I've learned that resilience isn't just an abstract concept," Khaled shared, his eyes reflecting a lifetime of wisdom. "It's a force that emerges from the depths of our being, enabling us to rise above challenges."

Their dialogue unfolded like a tapestry of shared insights, and as Khaled bid Arjun farewell, a sense of reverence lingered in the air. Khaled's symphony stood as a testament to the enduring power of resilience—a song that echoed through generations.

As Arjun's journey reached its zenith, he stood on the rooftop of his sanctuary—a place that had witnessed his evolution. The city stretched beneath him, a canvas painted with the stories of countless lives. The symphony of his own life had harmonized with the world's melodies, and in the intricate interplay, he had found his purpose.

In every connection he had formed, every heart he had touched, Arjun had learned that resilience was not just a solitary journey—it was a symphony that intertwined souls. The symphony had no conductor; it flowed through the collective spirit of humanity. And as he looked out over the city, Arjun knew that the symphony of resilience would continue, echoing through the ages, shaping the narratives of countless lives yet to unfold.

The night sky stretched above Arjun, a cosmic tapestry woven with stars. Their radiance, like distant notes, echoed the resilient symphony of the universe— an orchestra where he found his harmonious place. With each heartbeat, he sensed the timeless melody of endurance, a song that transcended the confines of time and space.

As the stars twirled in celestial dance, Arjun embraced the enduring refrain—the symphony of resilience that played on, an eternal anthem celebrating the indefatigable human spirit. It resonated in the quiet moments, echoed through the challenges, and pulsed in the victories. Arjun, a participant in this grand composition, marveled at life's ability to endure, thrive, and inspire others to join in the symphony.

His journey through the symphony of resilience unfolded as a testament to the profound strength within humanity. Adversity, once daunting, transformed into triumph. The intricate tapestry of Arjun's experiences continued to weave a melodic narrative, touching the hearts of those who listened—an ode to the indomitable spirit within us all.

One serene evening, Arjun found himself in a rustic village nestled amid rolling hills. The air carried the sweet perfume of blossoming flowers, and a tranquil serenity enveloped the surroundings. Meandering through the village square, Arjun was drawn to a scene that seemed to encapsulate the essence of resilience.

Beneath the shade of a tree, a young woman named Leela was engrossed in her craft, weaving intricate patterns on a loom. Arjun, captivated by the rhythmic dance of her fingers, approached with curiosity. Leela greeted him with a warm smile, her skilled hands conjuring a mesmerizing tapestry.

"This tapestry," Leela shared, "mirrors my journey—the symphony of resilience that has guided me through life's unpredictable rhythms."

At that moment, Arjun sensed a shared melody between them—a recognition of the universal symphony that connects every individual's unique journey. Leela's tapestry, a visual testament to resilience, became a living metaphor for the interconnected threads of strength woven through the fabric of existence.

Arjun's eyes traced the intricate patterns on Leela's tapestry, each thread narrating a saga of hardship, determination, and eventual triumph. "Your tapestry is a symphony in itself," he remarked, "a visual representation of the melodies that compose the journey of resilience."

Leela nodded, her fingers gently caressing the woven threads. "Just as each thread finds its place, every experience has shaped my symphony—the highs and lows, the challenges and the victories."

As the sun dipped below the horizon, casting a warm glow over the village, Arjun bid farewell to Leela. Their exchange of stories lingered in the air, etched in his heart like a timeless melody. He walked away, once again reminded that resilience was not merely a concept; it was a lived experience, a symphony echoing through the myriad paths of human existence.

Back in the heart of the bustling city, Arjun's impact radiated outward like ripples on water. The "Rhythms of Resilience" movement, born from his experiences, had grown beyond his wildest dreams. It reached corners of the world he had never imagined, becoming a sanctuary for individuals seeking solace—a symphony of shared experiences that transcended geographical boundaries.

In preparation for a global conference on resilience, Arjun found himself reflecting on the movement's profound impact. It was during this time that a letter arrived bearing the name David. David's narrative was one of transformation—a journey emerging from the depths of addiction and despair into a life infused with purpose and resilience. He expressed deep gratitude for Arjun's work, which had served as a guiding light on his arduous path.

Arjun's heart swelled with emotion as he read David's words. It was a poignant reminder that the symphony of resilience knew no boundaries—it was a melody that resonated with all those who chose to rise above their circumstances. The letter fueled Arjun's resolve as he prepared to share the collective symphony of stories at the upcoming conference, knowing that every tale, every note, contributed to the harmonious composition of the human spirit's enduring symphony.

On the conference stage, Arjun stood as a beacon, addressing an audience diverse in cultures, ages, and backgrounds. He shared the cadence of his journey—the soaring highs, the plunging lows, the moments of doubt, and the revelations that had reframed his perspective. His words wove a seamless symphony, each sentence a note contributing to the depth of his resonant message.

As his speech concluded, a young woman named Elena approached, tears reflecting the impact of Arjun's words in her eyes. "Your symphony has guided me through some of the darkest moments of my life. Your words have been a constant source of inspiration."

Arjun met Elena's gaze, a profound connection passing silently between them. "It's your resilience that inspires me," he replied. "Our symphonies intertwine, creating a harmony that resonates with the indomitable spirit within us."

In the ensuing months, Arjun's journey unfolded, and the "Rhythms of Resilience" platform evolved into a dynamic ecosystem of connection and growth. It became a space where stories intertwined, and resources were exchanged, and the symphony of resilience played on—a melody echoing with strength, courage, and hope.

One tranquil afternoon, seated by the river that had borne witness to his own moments of reflection, Arjun found a company in a young boy named Ayan. Having read Arjun's book, Ayan had been inspired to embark on his own journey. He spoke of dreams, fears, and a steadfast determination to overcome obstacles.

"The symphony of resilience," Ayan mused, "is like a river—it flows with a steady rhythm, carving its path through challenges and triumphs."

At that moment, as the river murmured its own timeless melody, Arjun saw the continuity of the symphony. It was a shared rhythm that connected lives, young and old, a testament to the enduring flow of resilience in every individual's journey.

Arjun's smile conveyed a deep understanding of Ayan's insight. "And just as a river connects diverse landscapes, the symphony of resilience unites us all in the journey of life."

As the sun dipped below the horizon, casting a warm glow over their surroundings, Arjun and Ayan shared a moment of quiet companionship. The symphony of their connection echoed in the tranquility of the evening. Ayan's presence served as a poignant reminder that the symphony of resilience knew no age boundaries—it was a melody that resonated with the hearts of all who dared to embrace the challenges life presented.

And so, as the world continued its ceaseless rotation, Arjun found himself at the epicenter of a symphony that transcended the constraints of time and space. Every experience, every encounter, and every shared moment of vulnerability and strength were woven together in a tapestry of resilience, spanning the vast canvas of humanity.

With each step he took, with every word he shared, Arjun contributed to the ongoing symphony of resilience—a melody that uplifted souls, kindled hope, and reverberated through the ages. As he cast his gaze to the horizon, he understood that the symphony would persist—a timeless composition celebrating the unyielding capacity of the human spirit to rise, endure, and to craft a harmonious masterpiece from the threads of life.

The Symphony of Resilience

Arjun's unwavering commitment to unraveling the symphony of resilience propelled him deeper into the intricate melodies woven into human stories. Each narrative he uncovered became a distinct note in the grand symphony of life, harmonizing to create a magnificent composition of strength, courage, and endurance. In the third part of "The Rhythms of Resilience," Arjun embarked on a mission to unveil the collective power of resilience. He sought to weave together stories from diverse communities, illustrating how this symphony resonated through societies, shaping their very essence.

With renewed vigor burning within him, Arjun set out on a profound exploration across the cultural tapestry of India. His journey led him to the remote corners of the Northeast, where he bore witness to the resilience of indigenous tribes grappling with the dichotomy of modernity and tradition.

Amidst the landscapes of Nagaland, Arjun discovered a group of women weavers who defied societal norms to safeguard their ancestral craft. Despite grappling with limited resources and access to markets, these women had woven together a thriving cooperative that empowered their entire community. Their collective effort served as a living testament to the symphony of unity, strength, and resilience echoing through the hills and valleys.

From the lush greens of the Northeast, Arjun's journey meandered to the arid expanses of Rajasthan. Here, he encountered the Bishnoi community—a tribe synonymous with an unwavering commitment to environmental conservation. Their profound reverence for nature and their steadfast dedication to protecting it became a unique manifestation of resilience. It was a resilience that extended beyond individual battles, encompassing the preservation of our planet's very essence.

As Arjun continued to uncover these stories, he realized that the symphony of resilience knew no geographical or cultural boundaries. It was a universal melody, playing on in the hearts and actions of individuals, communities, and societies across the tapestry of humanity. Each story added a new layer to the composition, creating a rich, diverse symphony that celebrated the strength inherent in the human spirit.

Wandering through the intricate tapestry of India, Arjun's journey intricately wove with the narratives of the nation's artisans. These skilled craftsmen, despite facing the unrelenting onslaught of mass production, persisted in breathing life into ancient art forms, standing as the custodians of the country's rich cultural heritage.

Arjun's path also intersected with the heart of communities—individuals who selflessly served, embodying resilience in its purest form. In rural

Karnataka, he encountered Dr. Shantha, a beacon of hope, dedicating her life to providing medical care to remote villages. Through adversity, her commitment to her patients became an embodiment of resilience, showcasing the profound impact one individual's determination could have on an entire community.

Yet, resilience wasn't confined to remote landscapes. Amidst the bustling urban jungles, Arjun met modern-day warriors navigating the complexities of contemporary life. Rahul, a young entrepreneur, emerged as one such embodiment of resilience. Having weathered multiple business failures, he used setbacks as stepping stones to pave his path to success—a living testimony that resilience was not merely about surviving but thriving against all odds.

As Arjun traversed through diverse communities, he couldn't help but draw parallels between human resilience and the cycles of nature. The steadfastness of trees, braving storms and droughts, mirrored the capacity of the human spirit to withstand life's challenges. The rhythmic harmony of nature's cycles—growth, decay, and renewal—served as a metaphor for the ebbs and flows of human resilience.

Arjun's fascination with the natural world led him to the iconic Banyan tree—a symbol of unwavering strength. The tree's aerial roots, branching out and creating new trunks, mirrored life's interconnectedness and resilience's innate ability to adapt and regenerate. In every twist of a branch and rustle of leaves, he found a silent anthem, a reminder that, like the Banyan tree, the symphony of resilience echoed through the interconnected threads of existence.

Amidst these profound encounters, Arjun sensed an intimate connection with the human spirit. He realized that resilience wasn't merely a personal attribute; it was a common thread that wove together diverse communities, transcending divisions of caste, creed, and culture.

Upon his return to Mumbai, Arjun was driven to share the inspiring tales of resilience he had uncovered. He curated a special section within "Rhythms of Resilience," illuminating the diverse stories of triumph from his journey.

The impact was profound. Readers resonated deeply with these stories, and many reciprocated by sharing their own personal journeys of resilience. "Rhythms of Resilience" transformed into a virtual sanctuary—a space for collective healing and growth.

This transformative influence extended beyond the digital realm. Collaborating with NGOs and community organizations, Arjun conducted workshops that unlocked the latent resilience and potential of underprivileged youth.

One particularly poignant workshop unfolded within the walls of an orphanage—a safe haven for children who had faced unfathomable hardships. Through art, storytelling, and mindfulness exercises, Arjun nurtured their innate resilience, kindling a spark of hope that transcended their difficult pasts.

Recognizing the paramount importance of building resilience in young minds, Arjun initiated collaborations with educational institutions. These partnerships integrated resilience-building modules into curricula, emphasizing emotional intelligence, self-compassion, and adaptability. The goal was to empower the next generation with the tools they needed to navigate life's challenges with grace and strength.

In the symphony of these collective efforts, Arjun witnessed the transformative potential of resilience—a force capable of not only shaping individual narratives but also uplifting entire communities and fostering a culture of shared strength and support.

In a world grappling with environmental crises and societal shifts, Arjun came to a profound realization— that resilience was the cornerstone of a compassionate and sustainable society.

The resonance of "Rhythms of Resilience" extended far beyond the borders of India, touching hearts globally. Collaborations with international organizations dedicated to mental health and community development catalyzed a global campaign. Through online summits, webinars, and social media initiatives, millions were reached, igniting a global movement rooted in compassion and understanding.

As the influence of the platform expanded, Arjun found himself at the helm of a community of change-makers and resilience advocates. Each member brought their unique story and perspective, enriching the symphony of resilience that echoed across continents.

Yet, amidst his global endeavors, Arjun remained connected to his personal journey of resilience. The call of the wilderness continued to draw him, and he sought solace in its embrace whenever his spirit needed rejuvenation. The dance between vulnerability and strength remained etched in his soul, a constant reminder that resilience was an ever-evolving tapestry.

While "Rhythms of Resilience" flourished, Arjun marveled at the transformation of a simple idea into a profound movement. Each new chapter brought an expanding collection of stories—tales that celebrated bravery, hope, and the relentless human spirit.

The symphony of resilience resounded through the ages, and Arjun's journey came full circle. To him, resilience wasn't just about extraordinary tales of victory; it was a celebration of humanity's ability to endure, evolve, and harmonize amidst the varied symphonies of life. As he looked back on his extraordinary voyage, he realized that the true beauty of resilience lay not just in individual triumphs but in the collective strength of the human spirit, creating a harmonious melody that echoed through the tapestry of time.

Resilience had become interwoven into the very fabric of Arjun's existence, guiding him through the darkest nights and brightest dawns. It was a melody that would accompany him as he embraced the journey ahead—a journey characterized by continuous growth, unceasing discovery, and an unwavering pursuit of purpose.

With a steadfast heart and a spirit that danced to the rhythms of resilience, Arjun welcomed the forthcoming chapter of "Rhythms of Resilience." This chapter promised deeper connections, shared purpose, and a symphony that would resound for generations to come.

The pages of Arjun's life turned with the rhythm of relentless exploration, each moment a new verse in the grand symphony of resilience. With every encounter, he uncovered a fresh note, a unique story that added depth and richness to the composition of human strength, perseverance, and hope. In the third part of "The Rhythms of Resilience," Arjun's quest led him to bridge the gaps between different stories, cultures, and communities, revealing the harmonious symphony that bound them all together.

With an unwavering determination, Arjun set forth on a journey that would take him beyond his own experiences. He embarked on an odyssey across the vibrant tapestry of India, seeking to understand how resilience manifested in diverse corners of the nation.

His footsteps led him to the remote and enchanting landscapes of the Northeast. Here, he encountered indigenous tribes whose resilience was an ode to the dance of tradition and modernity. Among the hills and valleys of Nagaland, Arjun met a group of women weavers who had transformed adversity into a tapestry of triumph. Through their cooperation, they not only revived traditional crafts but also empowered their community with a surge of strength and unity—a symphony of resilience that resonated through generations.

Leaving behind the lush green landscapes, Arjun ventured into the arid terrains of Rajasthan. Here, he crossed paths with the Bishnoi community—a testament to the unbreakable bond between resilience and environmental stewardship. Their unwavering commitment to protecting nature showcased a resilience that transcended personal battles and embraced the larger struggle of preserving the planet for future generations.

As Arjun continued his journey, he was drawn to the stories of India's artisans—guardians of heritage and culture. These craftsmen, often hidden away in the narrow lanes of bustling cities, breathed life into age-old traditions. Despite the tidal wave of mass-produced goods, their resilience kept ancient art forms alive, a testament to the symphony of cultural endurance.

His explorations took him to communities and individuals who personified resilience in its most profound forms. In the heart of rural Karnataka, Arjun encountered Dr. Shantha—a symbol of unwavering commitment in the face of adversity. Her determination to provide medical care to remote villages despite limited resources was a shining example of how resilience could permeate an entire community, lighting up the path to hope.

The urban landscapes, with their bustling energy, also revealed stories of resilience. Rahul, a young entrepreneur, emerged as a beacon of tenacity. His journey of overcoming multiple business failures underscored the symphony of resilience's transformative power—a reminder that setbacks could be stepping stones toward success.

In the tapestry of his explorations, Arjun couldn't help but draw parallels between human resilience and the patterns of nature. Just as trees weathered storms and droughts, the human spirit endured life's challenges. The natural world's rhythms—of growth, decay, and rebirth—echoed the ebb and flow of human resilience, where strength emerged from vulnerability.

Intrigued by the stories of the natural world, Arjun's curiosity led him to the iconic Banyan tree—a living symbol of unwavering strength. Its aerial roots, extending and giving rise to new trunks, mirrored the interconnectedness of life and the regenerative power of resilience.

As Arjun returned to Mumbai, his heart brimmed with a desire to share the symphony of resilience with a wider audience. He curated a dedicated section within "Rhythms of Resilience" to amplify the tales of triumph he had unearthed. The response was overwhelming. Readers resonated deeply with these narratives, and soon, the platform became a digital sanctuary—a place for collective healing, connection, and growth.

The transformative impact spilled beyond virtual realms as Arjun partnered with NGOs and community organizations. Through workshops, he ignited the spark of resilience in underprivileged youth, revealing their hidden potential.

An impactful workshop unfolded within the walls of an orphanage—a haven for children who had faced life's harshest challenges. Through art, storytelling, and mindfulness, Arjun nurtured their dormant resilience, igniting a flame of hope that transcended their past.

Understanding the urgency of nurturing resilience in young minds, Arjun collaborated with educational institutions. Resilience-building modules were integrated into curricula, emphasizing emotional intelligence, self-compassion, and adaptability.

In a world grappling with environmental crises and societal shifts, Arjun recognized that resilience was a cornerstone for a compassionate, sustainable society. The threads of resilience, woven into the fabric of individual and collective stories, became a guiding force toward a future where strength, empathy, and sustainability harmonized to create a resilient world for generations to come.

The resonance of "Rhythms of Resilience" transcended geographical boundaries, reaching hearts globally. Collaborations with international organizations dedicated to mental health and community development led to a global campaign. Through virtual summits, webinars, and social media, millions were reached, sparking a global movement of empathy and understanding.

As the platform's influence expanded, Arjun found himself at the helm of a community of change-makers and resilience advocates. Each individual contributed a unique story, enriching the symphony of resilience that reverberated across continents.

In the midst of these global endeavors, Arjun remained rooted in his own journey of resilience. The wilderness still called out to him, offering solace and renewal whenever he sought it. The dance of vulnerability and strength remained etched in his soul, a reminder that resilience was an ever-evolving tapestry.

As "Rhythms of Resilience" continued its harmonious journey, Arjun marveled at the transformation of a simple idea into a profound movement. With each new chapter, the collection of stories expanded—tales of courage, hope, and the enduring human spirit.

The symphony of resilience resonated through time, and Arjun's journey came full circle. Resilience wasn't just about exceptional tales of victory; it celebrated humanity's ability to weather storms, evolve, and harmonize with the varied symphonies of life.

The tapestry of resilience had woven itself into the very core of Arjun's existence, guiding him through the darkest nights and brightest dawns. It was a melody that would accompany him as he embraced the unwritten chapters—a journey of ongoing growth, discovery, and an unwavering pursuit of purpose. The symphony of resilience, both personal and collective, echoed through his life, a timeless melody that celebrated the beauty of the human spirit.

With a heart full of resolve and a spirit that danced to the rhythms of resilience, Arjun embraced the forthcoming chapter of "Rhythms of Resilience." This chapter promised deeper connections, shared purpose, and a symphony that would resonate for generations to come.

The symphony of Arjun's exploration into resilience escalated, weaving together the diverse notes of human stories into a harmonious composition. In the third part of "The Rhythms of Resilience," Arjun embarked on a transformative journey, fusing the threads of varied cultures and communities, revealing the unbreakable symphony that resonated across them all.

With unyielding determination, Arjun set forth on a voyage that stretched beyond his personal experiences. His path crisscrossed the vibrant mosaic of India, seeking to uncover how resilience manifested in its many facets.

He journeyed to the enchanting landscapes of the Northeast, where indigenous tribes lived amidst the hills and valleys. Among them, Arjun met a group of women weavers who had transformed adversity into triumph. Their cooperative not only revived traditional crafts but also kindled unity, infusing their community with resilience—a symphony of strength passed down through generations.

Transitioning from lush landscapes to arid terrains, Arjun found himself in Rajasthan. Here, he encountered the Bishnoi community—a living testament to the inseparable connection between resilience and environmental stewardship. Their unwavering commitment to preserving nature showcased a resilience that transcended personal battles, encompassing the broader struggle of safeguarding the planet for posterity.

As he continued his odyssey, Arjun was captivated by India's artisans—guardians of heritage and tradition. These craftsmen, often hidden within the labyrinthine streets of bustling cities, breathed life into ancient art forms. Their resilience upheld the cultural tapestry, weathering the storm of mass production—a reminder that within the symphony of adversity, resilience was a guiding note.

From communities to individuals, Arjun discovered stories that embodied the essence of resilience. In rural Karnataka, he met Dr. Shantha, a beacon of unwavering dedication. Despite resource limitations, she provided medical care to remote villages, demonstrating how resilience could extend its embrace, enveloping entire communities in hope.

The cacophony of urban life revealed yet more tales. Rahul, a young entrepreneur, emerged as a symbol of tenacity. His journey through multiple business failures was a reminder that the symphony of resilience transformed setbacks into stepping stones toward triumph.

As Arjun journeyed, he discerned parallels between the resilience of the human spirit and the patterns woven by nature. Just as trees stood firm in the face of storms, the human soul endured life's trials. The rhythm of nature's cycles mirrored the ebb and flow of human resilience—the strength born from vulnerability.

A beacon of nature's resilience, the iconic Banyan tree beckoned Arjun. Its aerial roots, extending and giving birth to new trunks, symbolized the interconnectedness of life and the regenerative power of resilience.

Back in Mumbai, a desire stirred within Arjun to share this symphony of resilience with a wider audience. He curated a dedicated section within "Rhythms of Resilience," amplifying the triumphant stories he had unearthed.

The response was profound. Readers embraced these narratives, and soon, the platform evolved into a sanctuary—a digital haven for collective healing, connection, and growth.

The transformative power extended beyond virtual boundaries as Arjun partnered with NGOs and community organizations. Through workshops, he lit the spark of resilience in underprivileged youth, revealing the dormant strength within them.

One workshop held within the walls of an orphanage breathed life into the children who had faced life's harshest storms. Through art, storytelling, and mindfulness, Arjun nurtured resilience, igniting a flame of hope that transcended their pasts.

With the urgency to instill resilience in young minds, Arjun joined forces with educational institutions. Resilience-building modules were integrated into curricula, highlighting emotional intelligence, self-compassion, and adaptability.

In a world grappling with challenges, Arjun recognized that resilience was the cornerstone of a compassionate, sustainable society.

"Rhythms of Resilience" resonated globally, touching hearts across continents. Collaborations with international organizations dedicated to mental health and community development led to a global movement. Virtual summits, webinars, and social media campaigns reached millions, sparking empathy and understanding.

As the platform's influence expanded, Arjun stood at the helm of a community of change-makers and resilience advocates. Each individual's story enriched the symphony that resonated across the world.

Amidst his global pursuits, Arjun remained anchored in his own journey of resilience. Nature's call beckoned him, offering solace and renewal whenever he sought it. The dance of vulnerability and strength remained etched in his soul, a constant reminder that resilience was an ever-evolving tapestry.

As "Rhythms of Resilience" continued its journey, Arjun marveled at the transformation of a simple idea into a profound movement. With each new chapter, the collection of stories expanded—tales of courage, hope, and the enduring human spirit.

The symphony of resilience echoed through time, and Arjun's journey came full circle. Resilience wasn't just about exceptional tales of victory; it celebrated humanity's ability to weather storms, evolve, and harmonize with life's symphonies.

The tapestry of resilience was woven into the very core of Arjun's existence, guiding him through the darkest nights and brightest dawns. It was a melody that would accompany him as he embraced the unwritten chapters—a journey of growth, discovery, and an unwavering pursuit of purpose.

With a heart full of resolve and a spirit that danced to the rhythms of resilience, Arjun welcomed the forthcoming chapter of "Rhythms of Resilience." This chapter promised deeper connections, shared purpose, and a symphony that would resonate for generations to come.

> Having faith in your path, embracing life's surprises, and trusting the process reveal unexpected opportunities

8

Echoes of Euphoria

April 16, 2022

The Quest for Bliss

Arjun's odyssey of resilience had traversed the landscapes of strength and vulnerability, forging a path that now beckoned towards an unexplored yearning—the quest for euphoria, a profound state of bliss that transcended the ordinary. As he delved into the unfolding pages of his own narrative in "Rhythms of Resilience," Arjun sensed the pulsating energy of a journey that would reveal the elusive secrets of this intangible treasure.

In his relentless pursuit of resilience, Arjun had unearthed the extraordinary within the ordinary, drawing strength from the crucible of adversity. However, with the turning of the pages into Chapter 8, his aspirations reached for something more profound—a connection with the core of existence, a dance with the universe's rhythm, and a surrender to life's symphony.

Euphoria, in Arjun's perspective, transcended the ephemeral peaks of happiness; it embodied a state of profound contentment independent of external circumstances. With a sense of purpose, Arjun embarked on a cross-cultural exploration, immersing himself in ancient teachings and seeking wisdom from those who had been cradled in euphoria's embrace.

The expedition unfolded in the mystical land of Rishikesh, where the Himalayas brushed against the heavens and the Ganges murmured age-old tales. Yogi Rajesh, a venerable sage renowned for his profound insights, became Arjun's beacon. Amidst the serenity of the ashram, Yogi Rajesh imparted, "Euphoria is the harmonious union of the mind, body, and soul. Through meditation and self-awareness, we can transcend the limitations of our human experience."

Draped in the tranquility of Rishikesh, Arjun immersed himself in Yogi Rajesh's teachings, sensing the delicate interplay between his breath and the universe. Within the embrace of the towering mountains, he discerned the heartbeat of the cosmos, finding himself seamlessly merging with its rhythmic cadence. The yogi's words echoed within him, a poignant reminder that euphoria was not a distant summit but an ongoing state of being.

From the serene embrace of Rishikesh, Arjun's sojourn carried him to the coastal allure of Kerala. Here, he encountered Mohini, a Kathakali dancer whose performances transcended the boundaries of language. Mohini's dance became a silent conversation with the soul, an expression that resonated directly with the heart. In the muted ambiance of the theater, as Mohini metamorphosed into characters of myth and legend, Arjun felt the enchantment of euphoria weave its magic.

Arjun's revelation unfolded—a realization that euphoria wasn't a solitary encounter but a shared symphony, a convergence of emotion and energy binding performer and audience. The applause that cascaded wasn't merely an accolade for the dancer; it stood as a homage to the euphoria birthed from the fusion of art, emotion, and connection.

Amma, his cherished grandmother, remained a steadfast beacon, radiating an aura of peace and acceptance that touched all in her presence. Under the sheltering branches of mango trees, her wisdom flowed like a gentle stream. "Euphoria isn't a destination; it's a melody that accompanies you. Embrace the notes of joy and sorrow, for together, they craft a symphony uniquely yours," she counseled with a gentle grace.

Observing Mumbai's vibrant streets, Arjun discerned life's rhythm—the laughter of children, the calls of street vendors, and the unity woven within diversity. Euphoria, he comprehended, wasn't confined to extraordinary moments; it was intricately interwoven with life's fabric. Every experience, every emotion, contributed a note to the symphony of existence.

Beneath the starlit canvas by the Arabian Sea, Arjun's quest crested. Euphoria wasn't an isolated chord but a harmonious blend of life's tones. The teachings of Yogi Rajesh, the dance of Mohini, and the wisdom of Amma entwined to lead him to this profound understanding. Euphoria, he now understood, wasn't an external conquest; it was an inner awakening.

As the waves murmured their timeless tales, Arjun's heart echoed with the symphony of his journey. The pursuit of euphoria wasn't the conclusion of a chapter;

it was the prologue to a life lived in synchrony with the universe. Each breath, each heartbeat, resonated as a note in the eternal melody of existence.

Arjun's quest for euphoria deepened as he immersed himself in two captivating stories, each unfolding a facet of this elusive state. The exploration continued, a journey fueled by the harmony of life's melodies and the wisdom acquired from the diverse voices encountered along the way.

Rishikesh's Whispers of Wisdom

In the tranquil cradle of Rishikesh, Yogi Rajesh's teachings unfolded like the delicate petals of a lotus, revealing the very essence of euphoria. Their dialogues often transcended the limitations of language, a silent understanding passing seamlessly between them. One evening, as they sat in quiet contemplation by the sacred Ganges, Arjun ventured to voice a question that had lingered in the depths of his heart: "Yogi Rajesh, can euphoria coexist with life's formidable challenges?"

Yogi Rajesh's eyes, deep pools of wisdom reflecting the moonlit waters, held a gaze filled with contemplation. "Life's challenges," he began, "resemble the currents of this sacred river. Euphoria isn't about avoiding them but navigating through with grace. Just as the river gracefully flows around obstacles, find your own flow amidst life's intricate twists and turns."

His words resonated within Arjun, creating ripples akin to the sacred river's gentle currents. Yogi Rajesh then wove a tale of a banyan tree—its roots, like steadfast anchors, embracing the earth. "Similarly," he advised, "cultivate roots of resilience within yourself. When life's storms arrive, you will stand firm, swaying with the winds but never uprooted."

As the moon cast its silvery glow upon their sanctuary, Yogi Rajesh led Arjun through a meditation—a journey inward. Amidst the subtle rustling leaves and distant chants, Arjun found himself immersed in a profound sense of peace. In the cocoon of stillness, he felt euphoria's gentle touch—the subtle whisper of the universe, the rhythmic pulse of existence. The moonlit meditation became a gateway, allowing Arjun to traverse the inner landscapes where euphoria awaited, not as an elusive destination but as a companion on the journey of self-discovery.

Amma's Unspoken Legacy

Arjun's contemplations often found solace in the presence of Amma, her being a soothing balm in the cacophony of life. One afternoon, beneath the sheltering branches of the mango trees, they shared a moment that etched itself deeply into his memory. "Amma, how can we find euphoria in life's chaos?" he queried, his gaze earnestly searching hers.

Amma's smile held a profound depth that transcended mere words. "Euphoria isn't elusive, my dear," she replied with a gentle wisdom. "It's the music that plays within when you dance to life's rhythm. Life, like the currents of a river, flows—sometimes calm, sometimes turbulent.

Embrace both, for they shape the unique melody of your existence."

Her fingers, like messengers of warmth and wisdom, gently brushed his cheek. "Euphoria resides in the simplicity of moments—a child's laughter, a shared meal, the tender touch of a loved one. Each of these is a note in the symphony of your life. Embrace them, and you'll dance to a melody that's uniquely yours."

Amma's words lingered in the air like a fragrant breeze, a comforting and guiding presence. Arjun comprehended that euphoria wasn't an unreachable star; rather, it manifested in the constellation of everyday moments that illuminated the vast sky of life.

As the chapter unfolded further, Arjun carried with him the resonance of Yogi Rajesh's meditations and Amma's teachings. They became his steadfast companions in moments of uncertainty, gently nudging him toward the path of euphoria—a journey marked by acceptance, resilience, and a profound joy found in the symphony of existence. Arjun's odyssey in search of euphoria would soon intersect with two stories that would forever shape his understanding of this elusive state, adding nuanced layers to his evolving melody of life.

Rishikesh's Serene Reverie

In the tranquil sanctuary of Rishikesh, Yogi Rajesh emerged as Arjun's sagacious guide along the intricate path to euphoria. Beneath the sprawling canopy of stars,

Arjun candidly unveiled his doubts, questioning, "Can euphoria truly be attained amidst life's relentless trials?"

Yogi Rajesh's eyes sparkled with the brilliance of ancient wisdom. "Euphoria isn't a flight from challenges, my friend; it's a harmonious dance of the mind, body, and soul in sync with the universe's rhythm. Just as the river gracefully navigates obstacles, so must you flow around life's challenges."

One twilight by the sacred Ganges, Yogi Rajesh imparted a meditation technique. As Arjun closed his eyes, the symphony of rustling leaves and distant chants blended into a celestial orchestra. Amidst this natural melody, he felt a profound calm—a reverberation of euphoria. Yogi Rajesh's voice echoed, "Within you, euphoria awaits. Release resistance and you'll discover it in the present moment."

Amma's Radiant Wisdom

In the embrace of memories, Arjun often sought solace in the wisdom of Amma, whose aura radiated tranquility. One day, beneath the sheltering mango trees, he expressed his yearning, "Amma, can euphoria be found amidst life's chaotic currents?"

Amma's eyes held a timeless depth, transcending the confines of mere moments. "Euphoria isn't a distant dream, my child," she replied, her voice echoing with the weight of profound experience. "It's a gentle breeze that caresses your soul when you embrace life's symphony.

Like the unyielding flow of a river, life's currents may alter, but your inner dance remains constant."

Her touch, as tender as a cherished melody, imprinted itself on his heart. "Euphoria resides in the simplicity of ordinary moments—an embrace, a shared laughter, a meal with loved ones. Cultivate these threads, for they weave the tapestry of your life."

Arjun's heart resonated with Amma's words. He came to understand that euphoria wasn't an isolated destination; rather, it was a constellation of moments, each illuminating life's expansive canvas.

As the unfolding chapter of his journey continued, Arjun carried within him the teachings of Yogi Rajesh and the legacy of Amma. They became his unwavering compass in life's storms, guiding him toward a dance of acceptance, resilience, and an ardent embrace of life's everyday treasures.

Embracing the Ephemeral

Arjun's exploration of the elusive realm of euphoria unfolded into a captivating odyssey, revealing a profound truth—the ethereal state couldn't be tethered or captured. Like morning dew on a fragile petal, euphoria emerged as a fleeting muse, casting its brilliance upon life's canvas only to be swept away by the whimsical winds of existence.

In the intricate web of this labyrinthine pursuit, Arjun encountered Anjali—a woman whose life bore the weight of shadows yet emerged as a phoenix from the ashes of adversity. Anjali's narrative unfolded like a chapter from an epic saga, where loss and resilience wove themselves into an intricate tapestry. Arjun found himself entangled in her story, the gravity of her experiences tugging at his heartstrings like an evocative melody.

Anjali wasn't merely a character; she embodied the struggles and triumphs of every reader. As her tale progressed, readers ceased to be mere spectators; they became compatriots in Arjun's journey, the echo of her words resonating within their own life experiences. Anjali's lessons were not delivered as sermons but as intimate conversations—a symphony of life's notes, weaving sorrows and joys in a tête-à-tête with readers.

In Anjali's resilience, a parallel emerged with the protagonist of a tragic opera—an indomitable spirit defying destiny's malevolent script. She had transmuted sorrow into an armor of strength, a metamorphosis that held Arjun in awe. Her insights carried the allure of an unsolved mystery, tempting readers with the promise of unlocking euphoria's well-guarded secrets.

Anjali's teachings were not mere dictations; they were profound interactions that resonated deeply with readers' souls. Every word became a brushstroke, painting vivid images of life's crescendos and descrescendos. As Arjun delved into her wisdom, readers, too, became introspective travelers, navigating through their own relationships with the transient nature of euphoria.

The invitation to the beach presented an uncharted realm of sensory experiences—a canvas painted with strokes of brilliance that allowed readers to savor the tang of brine, feel the granular texture of sand beneath their feet, and almost hear the symphony of waves caressing the shore. Anjali's metaphor, likening life to a relentless ocean, stirred the curiosity of readers, compelling them to plunge deeper into the vast ocean of understanding.

Arjun's metamorphosis unfolded as a captivating subplot, gaining momentum within the tapestry of the overarching narrative. Each revelation served as a spotlight, illuminating readers' personal introspections. Anjali's philosophy extended an inviting hand to readers, urging them to embrace life's kaleidoscope and compelling a reassessment of their own connection with the fleeting moments of euphoria.

As Arjun crossed paths with the reclusive monks, a new act in his journey unfolded against the backdrop of a secluded mountain monastery—a character in its own right, draped in mystique and beckoning readers to unravel its enigmatic depths. The mystical setting sparked a curiosity in readers akin to their fervor for enlightenment.

The teachings of the monks transcended mere monologues; they were profound dialogues with the universe. Arjun's interactions with them resembled scenes from an ancient script, where words carried the weight of timeless truths. Swami Aditya's utterances marked a climactic crescendo—readers' questions about euphoria found a voice resonating with their very thoughts.

The village became the canvas for the next chapter of Arjun's journey—a setting reminiscent of literary classics, evoking nostalgia and a yearning for discovery. The villagers were not mere characters; they embodied the avatars of readers' own quests for connection and meaning. The pages unfolded not only Arjun's interactions but also served as a reflective mirror, revealing readers' own emotions and experiences.

Nani's wisdom, delivered beneath a starlit sky, marked the pinnacle of a poignant scene—a moment laden with the weight of eternal truths. Readers' hearts were held captive as her words lingered, akin to an unforgettable melody. Nani's profound insights reverberated within readers, much like the timeless lessons of life that transcend the boundaries of time. Her philosophy emerged as a guiding beacon, casting light not only on Arjun's expedition but also on readers' individual quests for the ephemeral beauty of life.

In this rendition, the drama deepened, curiosity transformed into a burning ember, and engagement ignited into a fervent flame. Arjun's journey into the realm of euphoria retained its core essence, but now readers were integral participants, experiencing it through every word and emotion—a voyage that gripped them from the prologue to the epilogue. It was a journey not merely to be witnessed but to be lived.

Arjun's pursuit of euphoria had metamorphosed into a symphony of emotions, captivating both his heart and the souls of readers. The saga unfolded with a crescendo of feelings, each word resonating like a melodious note in the grand orchestration of existence.

As Arjun delved deeper into Anjali's world, her story ceased to be a mere narrative; it became an emotional odyssey that readers embarked on alongside him. Anjali's resilience became a wellspring of inspiration, her transformation a beacon of hope. Readers found themselves navigating the labyrinth of their own emotions, forging connections with Anjali's journey as if it were their own.

Anjali's philosophy, advocating the embrace of life's impermanence, transcended the realm of concept— it became a revelation that tugged at the very core of human existence. Readers were not just invited; they were compelled to step into her shoes to undergo life's highs and lows through her eyes. Every interaction with her felt like an intimate exchange, drawing readers into a shared exploration of the transient nature of existence.

The beach scene unfolded as a vivid canvas painted with sensory details, transporting readers to the very shore itself. The rhythmic sound of the waves, the gentle touch of the sand, and the salty taste of the sea breeze—all came alive in their minds, forging a visceral connection to the narrative. Anjali's metaphorical portrayal of life as an ocean resonated on a profound level, leaving readers contemplative about their own journeys amidst the ebbs and flows of existence.

As Arjun's journey led him to the secluded monastery, readers were enveloped in a world of mysticism and enlightenment. The monastery ceased to be merely a backdrop; it became a character shrouded in intrigue, a setting that kindled curiosity and wonder. Swami Aditya's teachings transcended the realm of monologues; they became dialogues, sparking a philosophical dance within the readers' minds compelling them to question the nature of euphoria and the essence of their own existence.

Arjun's experiences in the village constituted a chapter of contrasts—a picturesque backdrop against which readers could project their own desires for simplicity and connection. The village wasn't merely a setting; it became a reflection of readers' aspirations for a life less cluttered and more meaningful. Nani's wisdom acted as a conduit, connecting readers with the eternal truths of life's transience and encouraging them to embrace each fleeting moment with open hearts.

The storytelling project initiated by Arjun wasn't merely an endeavor within the narrative; it evolved into a narrative within the narrative—a tale of voices united by the common thread of euphoria. Readers bore witness to the birth of a movement that mirrored their own yearnings for self-discovery and connection. Their curiosity was piqued, and their engagement heightened as they followed the project's evolution with anticipation.

Meera's story emerged as a dramatic twist in Arjun's journey—a revelation that caught readers off guard and enveloped them in an aura of curiosity. Her triumph over adversity stood as a testament to the resilience of the human spirit, reflecting the readers' own battles with life's challenges. Meera's insights resonated deeply, encouraging readers to explore their individual paths to euphoria amidst the complexities of life.

As Arjun's expedition reached its culmination, readers transitioned from mere outsiders looking in to active participants in this journey of self-discovery and euphoria. The closing speech ceased to be Arjun's monologue; it transformed into a shared dialogue between him and the readers—a culmination of emotions and lessons that had been building throughout the section.

The readers' hearts swelled with pride and inspiration as Arjun stood on that stage, representing the apex of his growth, transformation, and the connections he had forged. Readers were not mere observers; they were fellow travelers who had walked this path with him, sharing in his triumphs and revelations.

In this rendition, the drama deepened, curiosity transformed into a burning ember, and engagement ignited into a fervent flame. Arjun's voyage into the realm of euphoria retained its core essence, but now readers were integral parts of this journey, experiencing it through every word and emotion—a voyage that gripped them from the prologue to the epilogue. It was a journey not merely to be witnessed but to be lived.

The narrative of Arjun's quest for euphoria continued to unfold, drawing readers into a world where emotions were not mere words on a page but waves that surged through their very beings.

Anjali's presence transcended a mere encounter; it became an intersection of two souls on parallel journeys. Her story held readers captive, inviting them to experience her losses and triumphs. The emotion in her voice became palpable, her perspective a beacon of light in the darkness of life's challenges.

Readers weren't mere spectators; they became Arjun's companions on this emotional rollercoaster. Anjali's teachings resonated with them, her insights serving as a mirror reflecting their own struggles with happiness and pain. The concept of embracing life's impermanence wasn't merely a theme; it was a whispered truth that stirred the curiosity of every reader.

As Arjun and Anjali sat by the beach, readers felt the grains of sand beneath their feet and heard the rhythmic symphony of the waves. Anjali's metaphor of life as an ocean transcended philosophical musings; it became a lingering melody, a riddle to be solved, a message to be decoded. Readers found themselves yearning to decipher life's patterns, much like Arjun himself.

The secluded monastery stood as a haven of mysteries, where readers sensed the weight of the mountains and heard the echoes of ancient wisdom. Swami Aditya's words didn't merely hang in the air; they resonated deep within readers' hearts. The idea of connecting with one's true self wasn't an abstract concept; it became a quest readers embarked on, following Arjun's footsteps up the mountain trails.

The village unfolded as a vibrant tapestry of life, woven with threads of humanity and interconnectedness. Readers weren't distant observers; they were drawn into the village's heartbeat, feeling the rhythm of its existence. Nani's wisdom became their own—a whisper that resonated through their minds as they contemplated the transient nature of life's joys and sorrows.

Arjun's storytelling project wasn't just a project confined to the pages; it became a bridge connecting readers with their own desire for connection and self-expression. Readers became stakeholders in this endeavor, their curiosity piqued, their engagement fueled as they envisioned themselves sharing their own stories.

Meera's revelation unfolded as a masterstroke—a twist that delicately tugged at the readers' emotions, leaving them eager for more. Her journey wasn't a mere tale; it became a reflection of the readers' own struggles, a mirror wherein they glimpsed their resilience and strength. Meera's insights ceased to be mere lessons; they transformed into seeds that planted curiosity in readers' minds, urging them to embark on their own paths to euphoria.

As Arjun's journey reached its zenith, the readers' hearts pounded in tandem with his. They transitioned from passive observers to active participants, caught up in a narrative that seamlessly merged with their own. The closing speech wasn't solely Arjun's address; it evolved into a collective conversation, a culmination of lessons learned, emotions felt, and the growth experienced by both characters and readers alike.

The readers' own quest for euphoria had been ignited, their curiosity stoked, and their engagement deepened. Arjun's voyage became theirs—a shared experience that left them inspired and introspective. They stood alongside him on that grand stage, their hearts echoing the rhythm of his journey, their souls dancing to the symphony of existence.

Having faith in your path,
embracing life's surprises, and
trusting the process reveal
unexpected opportunities

"

Challenges faced, mistakes
transformed into growth, and
strength earned over time create
a beautiful journey of evolution

9

The Harmony of Synchronicities

April 17, 2022

The Dance of Destiny

In the heart of Mumbai, a bustling metropolis pulsating with the rhythm of dreams and aspirations, Arjun found himself standing at the crossroads of his own existence. The city's towering skyscrapers reached for the heavens, casting long shadows on the streets below. Amidst this urban tapestry, Arjun's journey of self-discovery and transformation was poised to take an enchanting turn— one that would lead him into the mysterious realm of synchronicities.

On a misty morning heavy with the promise of rain, Arjun's feet carried him down an unfamiliar path. Lost in his thoughts, he deviated from his usual routine, unknowingly unraveling the fabric of his reality. Wandering, he stumbled upon a charming café tucked away like a hidden treasure. Drawn by an irresistible force, he entered, and that simple decision marked the first step in a sequence of events that would forever change his perspective on life.

Across the quaint café, their eyes met—Arjun's and hers. Maya, her name, possessed a radiant smile that seemed to emanate from a place of profound inner peace. Fate, it appeared, had orchestrated this serendipitous encounter. As they engaged in conversation, Maya's words carried a depth of wisdom that resonated with Arjun's restless soul.

"Life," Maya began, her eyes dancing with insight, "is a symphony of moments, a dance of energies that guides us along our destined path. Synchronicities are the universe's way of nudging us closer to our purpose if only we pay attention."

Captivated, Arjun felt the words resonate within him like a long-forgotten melody. Maya's tales of synchronicities—of chance meetings leading to profound insights, of signs and symbols pointing towards hidden truths—stirred something dormant within him. The concept that life was not a random sequence of events but an intricate choreography of destiny opened the door to a new dimension of understanding.

In the ensuing days, Arjun found himself finely attuned to the subtle whispers of the universe. The cosmos communicated through numbers—11:11, 777, and 222—materializing unexpectedly, as though orchestrating a cosmic ballet to seize his attention. Initially inclined to dismiss them as mere coincidences, their escalating frequency provoked a questioning within him, stirring contemplation on whether these numerical occurrences held a profound and deeper significance.

Gradually, he realized that synchronicities were not singular, isolated incidents but rather interconnected threads intricately weaving the fabric of his reality. Encounters with old friends providing precisely the guidance he needed, stumbling upon a book seemingly tailor-made for his current struggles, and even dreams imbued with messages that resonated deeply—all these elements began to unravel a grand design that governed his journey.

One luminous afternoon, seated in a park, Arjun's surroundings transformed into a canvas painted with the vibrant brushstrokes of synchronicity. A delicate and vibrant butterfly alighted gently on his hand, its wings fluttering gracefully—a dance of nature symbolizing transformation and rebirth. Nearby, the joyous laughter of a child filled the air as colorful balloons ascended toward the sky, akin to dreams taking flight.

The synchronicity inherent in these moments filled Arjun with a profound sense of wonder. Much like the butterfly shedding its cocoon to unveil its true beauty, he comprehended that he, too, needed to liberate himself from inhibitions and fears, allowing his spirit to soar in the currents of life. The universe, he realized, conveyed its messages not solely through numbers and events but through the intricate tapestry of existence itself.

Arjun's expedition took a profound turn as he delved into the teachings of venerable sages and ancient texts. Guided by the essence of synchronicities, he immersed himself in meditation and introspection, striving to deepen his connection with the symphony of the universe. The cacophony of the city's chaos gradually receded into the background as he embraced the dance of synchronicities, each step revealing a new layer of cosmic choreography.

In the presence of Swami Devananda, an elderly sage whose eyes held the wisdom of ages, Arjun discovered a profound guiding light. Beneath the swaying branches of a venerable banyan tree, Swami Devananda expounded on the profound significance of synchronicities in the spiritual journey. He shared insights into how the universe conspired to place the right people, lessons, and experiences on one's path, portraying each synchronicity as a harmonious note in the grand melody of life.

Arjun's perception underwent a transformative shift. Synchronicities, once perceived as mere coincidences, now revealed themselves as the universe's subtle language, communicating guidance and providing a roadmap toward higher consciousness. Swami Devananda's words resonated deeply within him, emphasizing that he was not merely a passive spectator in this symphony of existence but an integral player in its cosmic dance.

As the pages of time turned, Arjun's journey continued to unfold in symphonic harmony. The Euphoria Stories Project, a venture sparked by synchronicity, burgeoned into a global movement, disseminating resilience and joy across borders. His book, "Rhythms of Resilience," emerged as a beacon of hope for those seeking meaning in their struggles, with its words intricately woven into the tapestry of synchronicities.

Guided by Swami Devananda's profound wisdom, Arjun's connection with the dance of synchronicities deepened. He realized that this dance wasn't confined to extraordinary moments; it was a constant undercurrent, seamlessly connecting every facet of existence.

Each synchronicity served as a gentle reminder that he was an integral part of a larger narrative, a narrative where every encounter and event held a purpose.

Standing before the boundless expanse of the sea, Arjun felt a profound resonance with the universe's rhythm. He marveled at the constellations above, akin to ancient storytellers etching tales of destiny across the night sky. The dance of synchronicities had metamorphosed his life into a living symphony—a composition resonating with resilience, grace, and interconnectedness.

Within the pages of existence, Arjun unfolded the realization that synchronicities were not random occurrences; they were the gentle whispers of the universe guiding him toward his true essence. Standing on the precipice of the horizon, he acknowledged that his journey was an ongoing saga. The symphony of synchronicities would persist, inviting him to waltz with the cosmos, urging him to surrender to the rhythm of life's grand composition.

Arjun's existence had metamorphosed into a tapestry interwoven with the delicate threads of synchronicities. Each moment, each encounter, became a note contributing to the grand symphony of life, harmonizing with the universe's rhythm. The city, once perceived as chaotic, now pulsed with concealed patterns, inviting him to decipher its hidden melodies.

Guided by Swami Devananda, Arjun embarked on a voyage of self-discovery that transcended the confines of the physical world. Meditation evolved into a bridge connecting his conscious mind with the realm of the unseen—a space where synchronicities manifested in their purest form. Through this practice, he realized that synchronicities weren't solely external occurrences but reflections of his inner landscape.

In the hush of meditation, Arjun learned to attune himself to the whispers of his soul. He found harmony with the symphony of his own heartbeats, each pulse resonating with the universal rhythm. Delving deeper, he encountered moments of profound clarity, as if the universe itself communicated with him through the language of synchronicities.

One evening, bathed in the serenity of the sea while immersed in meditation, Arjun witnessed a breathtaking sunset—a spectacle where the sky transformed into a canvas painted with hues of gold and crimson. A lone seagull gracefully soared across the horizon, its silhouette a dance of elegance against the backdrop of nature's masterpiece. In that profound moment, Arjun realized that he was an integral part of a larger choreography—an intricate dance where every living being played a unique role.

As Arjun's connection with synchronicities deepened, he started to perceive their influence not only in his personal journey but also in the lives of those surrounding him. He observed friendships rekindled by chance encounters, strangers providing timely words of encouragement, and events unfolding in a way that defied conventional logic yet seamlessly wove together.

During a visit to an ancient bookstore tucked away in a forgotten corner of the city, Arjun stumbled upon a time-worn text that expounded on the interconnectedness of all life. Its pages resonated with the essence of synchronicities, portraying them as threads intricately woven into the fabric of existence by a cosmic weaver. Arjun realized that the dance of synchronicities wasn't confined to his individual story; it was an elaborate narrative shared by all beings.

Surrounded by friends and fellow seekers, Arjun observed that synchronicities became even more pronounced. Conversations flowed effortlessly, ideas collided and merged, and solutions unfolded as if guided by an unseen hand. He comprehended that when individuals aligned their intentions and energies, the dance of synchronicities transformed into a symphony of collaboration and co-creation.

As the years unfolded, Arjun's exploration journey expanded beyond the city's borders. He ventured into remote villages, climbed towering mountains, and delved into tranquil forests. Everywhere he traversed, he encountered the subtle footprints of synchronicities—the wind whispering its secrets, the rustling leaves, the melodious song of a bird—all conspiring in harmony with the universe.

During his extensive travels, Arjun encountered individuals whose lives had been touched by synchronicities in extraordinary and miraculous ways. A farmer recounted a chance encounter that led to the discovery of drought-resistant seeds, transforming the fortunes of his entire village. An artist shared the tale of a vivid dream, inspiring a masterpiece that resonated deeply with many. These stories served as powerful affirmations, reinforcing Arjun's belief that synchronicities transcended logic, acting as expressions of the universe's boundless wisdom.

Within the grand tapestry of existence, Arjun came to a profound realization—synchronicities were invitations to dance with the unknown, to embrace the magic intricately woven into the fabric of reality. Life's symphony, he understood, wasn't confined to predetermined notes; rather, it was a collaborative composition in which he played the dual roles of conductor and participant.

On a starlit night, standing at the precipice of a cliff overlooking the city's twinkling lights, Arjun felt an overwhelming sense of gratitude. The dance of synchronicities had guided him through life's labyrinth, unveiling hidden paths and truths. He marveled at the intricate connections that had led him to this very moment—a culmination of countless synchronicities.

Swami Devananda's enduring presence remained a guiding light in Arjun's life, a testament that the dance of synchronicities wasn't a mere concept but a lived experience—a continuous conversation with the universe. The sage's words echoed in his mind: "Synchronicities are the melodies of destiny, the orchestration of the cosmos guiding us back to our true nature."

As Arjun stood on the brink of a new chapter, he carried with him the symphony of synchronicities as a guiding force. He recognized that his journey was an ongoing composition, a dance of co-creation with the universe. With each step, he embraced the magic inherent in the ordinary, appreciating the beauty that emerged from the unseen.

In a world fraught with chaos and uncertainty, Arjun had unearthed the revelation that synchronicities were the invisible threads connecting him to the vast cosmic web. The dance of synchronicities had led him to a profound understanding—that life was not a solitary journey but a collaborative masterpiece, a symphony where every note played an indispensable role.

As Arjun gazed into the horizon, where the sky met the sea in an eternal embrace, he knew that the dance of synchronicities would persist in guiding him. It invited him to surrender to the music of the universe. His heart swelled with purpose, for he was no longer a mere spectator; he had become an active participant in life's grand dance—a dance harmonizing with the rhythm of the cosmos, leading him to the deepest realms of his own soul.

Embracing the Flow

As the river of time flowed steadily, Arjun found himself embraced by its constant motion, his journey evolving into a rich tapestry woven by the hands of time. His reputation burgeoned, not merely as a leader in marketing transformation but as a luminary whose name became synonymous with the dance of synchronicities. The world opened its arms to him, and in return, he shared the wisdom of his heart, disseminating the truths he had gleaned from the universal choreography of synchronicities.

His second literary offering, "Synchronicities Unveiled," transcended borders and languages, moving beyond mere words to evoke a resonance deep within the human psyche. The cover, adorned with intricate patterns resembling constellations, beckoned readers to explore the galaxies of their own experiences. In it, Arjun masterfully intertwined storytelling with philosophy, revealing the dance between the mundane and the metaphysical.

The pages of the book carried readers through corridors of epiphany and passages of wonder, leading them to the profound realization that synchronicities were not the exclusive domain of mystics and seers but an intrinsic aspect of every life. Arjun's eloquence created bridges between the seen and the unseen, igniting sparks of curiosity and introspection.

Each chapter was a journey—a voyage through the lives of those who had brushed against the fabric of synchronicity. Arjun unveiled stories of ordinary individuals thrust into extraordinary circumstances by the gentle yet decisive nudges of the universe. He recounted how the threads of fate converged in the most unassuming moments, forever altering their courses and setting them on paths lit by the cosmic dance.

The success of "Synchronicities Unveiled" surpassed even Arjun's most optimistic expectations. It graced the upper echelons of bestseller lists around the world, adorning bookstore displays like a guiding star. Its contents were more than words; they were invitations to embark on a journey into the realm of the unknown, with synchronicities as the compass guiding readers through the cosmic dance of life.

Arjun's radiant presence illuminated television screens, radio waves, and digital platforms. His interviews were not mere discussions; they were symphonies of thought conducted with grace and humility. Listeners were drawn to his words like moths to a flame, feeling a resonance that transcended the auditory and echoed in the chambers of their hearts.

In a conversation that reached millions, a journalist questioned the authenticity of synchronicities. Arjun's response was a testament to his depth of understanding. "Synchronicities are not mystical occurrences limited to a chosen few," he calmly elucidated. "They are the universe's subtle invitations to expand our perspectives and embrace the interconnectedness of all existence."

Arjun's book tours became cultural events, attracting diverse crowds united by a shared curiosity about the dance of synchronicities. People stood in lines that snaked around blocks, clutching their copies as if holding talismans of hope and discovery. Arjun's interactions with his readers were genuine exchanges, each person leaving with more than an autograph—they departed with an ignited spark, ready to dance to the rhythm of their own synchronicities.

Online communities flourished, becoming gardens where people planted the seeds of their synchronicity stories and watered them with shared experiences. Arjun was an active participant, offering insights that transcended the virtual realm. "Your stories are the constellations that illuminate the night sky of human existence," he commented, acknowledging the beauty of each individual's journey.

The years unfolded like brushstrokes on a canvas, each stroke adding depth and complexity to Arjun's life. His children, now grown into individuals of their own, embraced his teachings with a blend of pride and gratitude. They spoke of how their lives had been shaped by the dance of synchronicities that had illuminated their father's journey.

In the midst of it all, Meera remained his rock, his partner who had not only shared the dance but had also contributed her own choreography to their shared existence. Their love story was a testament to the enduring power of connection, fortified by synchronicities that wove their destinies together like threads in a cosmic tapestry.

The Euphoria Festival had evolved into a global phenomenon, a celebration that resonated with the hearts of those who sought conscious living, art, and music. The festival's central message was simple yet profound—the dance of synchronicities was an intricate part of life, and embracing it led to boundless joy and transformation.

One day, as the festival pulsed with energy and the stage awaited him, Arjun felt a profound sense of alignment with the universe's rhythm. He gazed at the sea of faces before him, recognizing the universality of human longing for connection and purpose.

"I stand before you today not as an expert but as a fellow dancer in this cosmic ballet," Arjun began, his voice a resonant melody that echoed through the hearts of those present. "Synchronicities are not fleeting moments; they are the universe's invitations to partner with the cosmos in a dance of discovery."

The audience listened in rapt attention, captivated by Arjun's presence and the authenticity with which he shared his personal journey. He painted a vivid tapestry of synchronicities, each thread connecting humanity in a grand tapestry that spanned time, space, and the essence of existence.

"Let us embrace uncertainty, for within it lies the canvas where synchronicities paint their masterpieces," Arjun proclaimed, his arms outstretched, weaving a connection between the gathered audience and the vast cosmos. This was not just a speech; it was an invocation, a call to dance with life itself. "Together, let's surrender to the cadence of synchronicity, letting it carry us towards the undiscovered realms of our individual destinies."

The applause that followed was not mere clapping; it was a symphony of agreement, an acknowledgment that a universal truth had been unveiled. Stepping away from the podium, Arjun felt the warmth of accomplishment radiating from his heart. His mission had been fulfilled—to invite the world to experience the dance of synchronicities in all its vibrant shades.

As the festival lights painted the night sky, Arjun raised his gaze, feeling the gentle caress of the breeze against his skin. It was as if the cosmos itself acknowledged his role in its grand dance. With a smile that mirrored the stars, he joined the ebullient crowd, ready to embrace every twist, turn, and leap that the cosmic choreography had yet to unveil.

For Arjun, life wasn't a mere sequence of events; it was a grand dance—a symphony of synchronicities pulsating through every heartbeat, every breath, and every soul.

His impact extended far beyond the boundaries of literary circles. Arjun's teachings echoed through boardrooms, classrooms, and living rooms alike, sparking conversations that delved beyond the superficial into the profound. Synchronicities were no longer whispered secrets; they had become vibrant threads intricately woven into the fabric of daily life. People began to see the beauty in uncertainty, finding inspiration in the unpredictable rhythms of existence.

Arjun's journey had transcended the limitations of a single individual; it had become a collective exploration, a shared revelation that encouraged each person to unravel the mysteries of their own existence. The ripple effect of his words reached corners of the world untouched by conventional wisdom, inspiring a global embrace of life's intricate dance.

And so, as Arjun moved through the jubilant crowd, he wasn't just a speaker; he was a fellow dancer, navigating the cosmic choreography alongside every person he touched. The festival continued, not merely as a celebration of a moment but as an ongoing tribute to the endless dance of synchronicities that painted the tapestry of human experience.

Arjun's influence expanded far beyond the written word. International symposiums and conferences extended invitations to him, recognizing him not just as a thought leader but as a harbinger of transformation. His keynote speeches were not mere presentations; they were immersive experiences that ignited minds and kindled spirits.

In a grand gathering of global thinkers, innovators, and change-makers, Arjun stood on a stage that served as his canvas. His words, more than mere sentences, were strokes of inspiration painting a vivid portrait of synchronicities' profound role in human evolution.

"Synchronicities are the melodies that underscore the composition of our lives," Arjun declared, his eyes ablaze with the fire of conviction. "When we tune in to their frequency, we unlock doors that lead to our own potential and purpose."

His words weren't just spoken; they were harmonious chords that struck deep within the hearts and minds of those in the audience. The realization dawned that synchronicities were not ethereal wisps but tangible guides, helping them navigate the labyrinth of existence.

Amidst the corridors of these gatherings, conversations buzzed with an energy that transcended small talk. Attendees shared stories of serendipities that had led them to crossroads they never knew existed. Arjun's presence had ignited a collective awareness—a recognition of the threads that wove their lives together.

Through his tireless efforts, Arjun forged collaborations with thought leaders across diverse fields. Scientists, artists, philosophers—they all found common ground in the dance of synchronicities. Dialogues flourished, giving rise to groundbreaking discoveries that blurred the lines between the seen and the unseen.

In these intellectual and spiritual gatherings, Arjun was not just a speaker; he was a catalyst for transformation. The atmosphere crackled with the excitement of minds opening to new possibilities, and the ripple effect of these experiences spread far beyond the confines of the conference halls.

As Arjun continued his journey, his impact on the collective consciousness deepened. The symphony of synchronicities, once a subtle melody, now echoed loudly in the minds of those who had the privilege of listening. The world was awakening to the interconnected dance of life, and Arjun stood at the forefront—a beacon of inspiration guiding humanity toward a higher understanding of its purpose and potential.

One of the most memorable interactions in Arjun's journey unfolded in a conversation with an acclaimed neuroscientist. Together, they delved into the intricate intersection of science and spirituality, exploring the neural pathways that might be illuminated by the dance of synchronicities. Arjun eloquently conveyed that the symphony of the universe resonated not just in the cosmos but within every neuron and synapse, suggesting a profound connection between the external and internal worlds.

As the years advanced, Arjun's explorations took him to the heart of ancient civilizations. Walking amidst ruins that whispered tales of synchronicities experienced by those who had come before, he found himself in Egypt beneath the watchful gaze of the pyramids. There, Arjun contemplated the role of synchronicities in shaping human history, sensing an ancient dance that transcended time.

Standing before the towering stones of Stonehenge, Arjun felt the pulse of the earth beneath his feet. He envisioned the countless generations who had marveled at the celestial choreography enacted above these ancient stones, finding in them a reflection of their own life rhythms. It was as if the stones held the key to unlocking the secrets of synchronicities embedded in the very fabric of existence.

During his journey, Arjun stumbled upon a sacred monastery nestled in the heart of the Himalayas. The monks, attuned to the dance of synchronicities, welcomed him as a kindred spirit. In their conversations, which transcended words, Arjun discovered the universal language that connected all beings—a language spoken in the silent whispers of synchronicity.

One evening, as the sun dipped below the horizon, painting the sky with hues of gold and crimson, Arjun sat in meditation with the monks. He felt the energy of the mountains enveloping him, a reminder that synchronicities were not just fleeting moments but eternal companions on the journey of self-discovery.

"Life is the canvas, and synchronicities are the brushstrokes that add depth and meaning," a venerable monk whispered, his eyes reflecting lifetimes of wisdom. "As you dance with synchronicities, you become a co-creator of the masterpiece of existence." The words echoed in the mountainous silence, imprinting a profound truth on Arjun's soul—an understanding that the dance of synchronicities wasn't just a philosophical concept; it was a lived experience that connected the past, present, and future in a timeless continuum.

Arjun's journey unfolded beyond the grand stages and into remote villages, where ancient traditions and wisdom were passed down through generations like precious heirlooms. Here, he discovered that the dance of synchronicities was not a new phenomenon but an age-old wisdom encoded in cultures worldwide. From indigenous tribes to ancient civilizations, synchronicities have always been an integral part of the human experience.

Sitting around campfires and sharing meals with villagers, Arjun realized that the dance of synchronicities was a universal language that transcended barriers of language and geography. It became evident that, beneath the surface, every human heartbeat to the rhythm of the cosmic dance, an invisible thread weaving together the tapestry of humanity.

With every step of his journey, Arjun's awareness of synchronicities deepened. No longer mere coincidences, he recognized that they were orchestrated messages from the universe—a reminder that he was intricately connected to a vast, cosmic tapestry. Each synchronicity whispered a deeper truth, guiding him along a path of self-discovery.

As the years unfolded, Arjun's presence became synonymous with the dance of synchronicities. His impact on the world was not measured by accolades or awards but by the transformation he ignited within countless lives. His legacy wasn't written in stone but etched in the hearts of those who had danced with him to the cosmic rhythm, embracing the profound interconnectedness of all things.

On a quiet evening, as Arjun stood on a cliff overlooking the vast expanse of the ocean, he marveled at the journey he had undertaken. The same ocean that had once whispered secrets to him now echoed with the harmonious laughter of synchronicities. With a heart full of gratitude, he whispered a silent thank you to the universe—for the dance, the lessons, the connections. His journey was a never-ending one, an ever-evolving partnership with the cosmos, a continuous exploration of the intricate dance that wove together the threads of existence.

Arjun closed his eyes and surrendered to the cosmic dance as the sun dipped below the horizon, casting a tapestry of colors across the sky. Every heartbeat, every breath, became a step in the eternal choreography of synchronicities—a dance that would continue to echo through the ages, guiding souls toward their destinies.

Arjun's journey of synchronicities evolved into a mesmerizing odyssey that captivated hearts across continents. His presence radiated a magnetic pull, drawing people from all walks of life into the orbit of his wisdom. The world began to recognize him not just as a bestselling author but as a modern-day sage—a beacon of light in a world yearning for deeper meaning.

Invitations poured in from prestigious institutions, each one seeking to host Arjun as a guest lecturer. Universities, renowned for their pursuit of knowledge, embraced his teachings as a bridge between academia and spirituality. Arjun's lectures weren't just intellectual discourses; they were invocations that sparked flames of curiosity and self-discovery.

In a packed lecture hall, Arjun stood before a sea of eager faces, each one hungry for insight. The air was electric with anticipation as he began to speak. "Synchronicities are the whispers of the universe, inviting us to partake in the cosmic dance," he proclaimed, his voice resonating with an innate truth that touched every heart.

His words wove a tapestry of understanding, connecting dots that had long remained elusive. Arjun shared stories of synchronicities that had guided him to uncharted territories of consciousness, urging his audience to recognize the same potential within themselves.

After his talk, a young student approached Arjun, her eyes ablaze with excitement. "You've opened a door within me that I never knew existed," she confessed. "I feel like I've been handed a treasure map to navigate the labyrinth of life." Arjun smiled, recognizing that, at that moment, another soul had begun its own dance with synchronicities, ready to explore the vast and uncharted territories of their own existence.

Arjun smiled, acknowledging the spark ignited within her. "We are all explorers in this grand journey," he replied. "Synchronicities are the constellations that guide us through the night."

Beyond the lecture halls, Arjun's influence extended to digital realms. His podcast, aptly named "Synchronicity Chronicles," became a global sensation. With each episode, he shared captivating narratives of synchronistic encounters, inviting listeners to step into the river of cosmic flow.

In one episode, Arjun recounted his encounter with a reclusive artist who had spent decades creating intricate mandalas. Through their conversation, he unraveled the intricate threads that connected the artist's work to the dance of synchronicities. Listeners marveled at the realization that even art could be a vessel for the universe's messages.

The podcast fostered a community of seekers who exchanged their own stories of synchronicities. Emails and messages poured in from individuals who had witnessed the magic of divine orchestration in their lives. Arjun's digital presence transcended geographical boundaries, uniting souls in a shared exploration of the cosmos' mysteries.

Amidst his global engagements, Arjun found solace in the embrace of nature. He embarked on solitary retreats to remote landscapes, seeking communion with the elements. In the heart of lush forests, he discovered a world pulsating with synchronistic energy—a reminder that the universe's dance was not confined to human interactions alone.

One moonlit night, while sitting beside a roaring waterfall, Arjun felt a presence—a spiritual kinship with the unseen. He closed his eyes and allowed himself to be enveloped by the symphony of water and wind. At that moment, he experienced a profound revelation—a realization that synchronicities were not just external guides but reflections of the internal symphony of his own soul. The waterfall, the moonlight, and the rustle of leaves became notes in a cosmic melody, echoing the interconnected dance of the universe within the depths of his being.

The profound beauty of synchronicities lies not only in their eloquent language but in their universal adaptability, seamlessly weaving through diverse cultures, languages, and belief systems. Arjun, a sage whose teachings transcended religious boundaries, became a living bridge, emphasizing that beneath the surface of varied traditions, a common truth bound humanity—the truth of interconnectedness and divine orchestration.

Amidst the pulse of urban life and the tranquility of untouched landscapes, Arjun's life unfolded as a magnificent tapestry. Each thread, delicately interwoven with the golden strand of synchronicities, depicted a narrative that resonated with seekers across the spectrum. His presence wasn't just an invitation to abandon material pursuits; it was a call to embrace the cosmic rhythms and recognize the symphony echoing in every heartbeat.

Decades wove their patterns into the fabric of Arjun's journey, revealing a mentor who, instead of resting on past laurels, evolved with the changing cadence of life. His guidance wasn't confined to a single generation; it transcended time, reaching out to new seekers embarking on their personal quests for truth. For Arjun, the dance of synchronicities wasn't merely a wondrous voyage; its true magic lay in the awakening it kindled—a realization that every step taken was a step toward the divine.

Standing on a cliff, the world spread beneath him like an intricate mosaic, Arjun heard an internal whisper, "Your journey has come full circle." His gaze swept across the horizon, feeling the dance of synchronicities as an eternal waltz stretching beyond the boundaries of time and space.

In a moment of profound surrender, he closed his eyes, allowing the cosmic current to embrace him. It wasn't just an individual's journey; it was a thread woven into the eternal symphony resonating through the cosmos.

As the sun dipped below the horizon, casting a palette of amber and rose across the world, Arjun sensed that his dance with synchronicities was an everlasting one. It wasn't a mere dance but a cosmic choreography that would echo through ages, urging souls to awaken to the enchantment within and embrace the cosmic guidance steering them toward their destinies.

66

Flowing with life's rhythm, recognizing its signs, and accepting fate create a harmonious dance with the universe"

99

10

The Pattern of Resilience

June 6, 2022

The Melody of Endurance

In a world that often sought the quick and the convenient, Arjun emerged as a bastion of resilience, a living testament to the enduring power of the human spirit. The years had etched profound lines on his face, each wrinkle telling a story of challenges faced and conquered. He had become not merely an individual but a symbol of strength, a lighthouse that guided others through their storms.

As the sun gracefully dipped below the horizon, casting a warm golden glow over the city, Arjun found himself enveloped in a familiar haven—a quaint café that had witnessed the ebb and flow of countless conversations and shared moments. The fragrant tendrils of his coffee intertwined with the memories that lingered in the air, creating a tapestry of experiences.

Rahul, Arjun's dearest friend, took his seat at the table. The bond they had forged during their shared journey of grief had evolved into an unbreakable connection. Rahul's eyes held a blend of gratitude and admiration as he spoke, "Arjun, sometimes I find myself pondering how you managed to persist, to stand firm in the face of adversity."

Arjun's gaze met Rahul's, a serene smile playing on the edges of his lips. "Resilience," he replied, his voice a steady and calming force, "is akin to a melody that plays within us. It's not about evading the storms but about dancing in the rain."

Their conversation gracefully meandered through the corridors of time, settling on the early days of their friendship when the pain of loss was a raw and unrelenting wound. "I recall the moment you appeared at my doorstep," Rahul shared, his voice carrying the weight of emotion. "You didn't come bearing solutions, but your mere presence was a balm to my soul."

Arjun nodded, revisiting the unspoken understanding they had shared—a silent acknowledgment of the profound healing power inherent in companionship. "We frequently underestimate the strength that emanates from simply being there for each other," he reflected.

Arjun's journey of resilience resembled more of a winding path than a straight line. Life's challenges had, at times, threatened to engulf him in their weight. Yet, whenever he felt on the verge of drowning, the universe gently nudged him toward the surface, underscoring the dance of synchronicities that guided him.

One particular instance remained etched in his memory—a period when he questioned the very purpose of his struggles. It was during this nadir that a letter from a reader arrived, bearing words that cut through his despair: "Your journey has given me the strength to face my own battles. Your words are a reminder that even in the darkest times, there's a glimmer of light."

The synchronicity of receiving such a letter precisely when he needed it most fortified Arjun's belief in the interconnectedness of all life. Explaining this to Rahul, he said, "Synchronicities are like guideposts on our journey. They remind us that we are not alone—that the universe conspires to help us rise above our challenges."

Arjun's professional trajectory had also weathered its share of storms. Setbacks had tested his patience and resolve. However, with each stumble, he delved into the reservoir of resilience within him, transforming obstacles into stepping stones toward growth.

A particular project echoed in his thoughts—a seemingly irreparable venture where his team faced an onslaught of challenges, and pressure loomed large. Arjun, however, approached the situation not as an insurmountable hurdle but as an opportunity for transformation. Gathering his team, he spoke with unwavering determination, "Let's view these challenges as opportunities. Together, we'll find a way to turn this around."

Their collective efforts and unyielding determination had not only salvaged the project but also woven tighter the threads of connection within the team. "Resilience," Arjun imparted to Rahul, "is not just about bouncing back. It's about bouncing forward with newfound wisdom." Rahul reclined in his chair, his eyes mirroring a newfound comprehension. "You've shown me that resilience isn't about sidestepping pain but about transforming it into something meaningful."

Arjun's gaze shifted to the horizon, where the sun now lingered as a mere sliver of gold. "Exactly," he affirmed. "Just as a sculptor molds raw stone into a masterpiece, resilience shapes us into something more beautiful than we could have envisioned."

As the evening unfolded, the café's lights enveloped them in a warm glow, creating a cocoon of shared stories and unspoken truths. Arjun's odyssey of resilience had taught him that life's challenges weren't obstacles to surmount but rather notes in the symphony of existence—a melody of endurance binding them all.

Rahul, too, had unearthed his own wellspring of strength through their friendship. Both realized that the dance of synchronicities was a rhythm guiding them toward growth, imparting the understanding that resilience was not merely a trait but a way of life—a path leading to deeper comprehension, compassion, and connection.

As they bid farewell that evening, their embrace carried the warmth of a bond forged in the crucible of adversity. Arjun departed, his steps purposeful and unwavering, cognizant that his journey of resilience was an ongoing narrative. Within him, he bore the wisdom of synchronicities' dance and the enduring melody of endurance.

The city's skyline painted itself in hues of orange and pink as Arjun traversed familiar streets. Amidst the urban chaos, he found solace—a testament to his resilience. Each measured step echoed the rhythm of his journey, a journey that had schooled him in the art of transforming adversity into strength.

As Arjun stepped into the tranquil park, a haven for countless moments of introspection, his mind retraced its steps to a time when his path was cloaked in uncertainty. The loss of his parents had gouged a void seemingly insurmountable, a darkness threatening to engulf him.

It was during those days of soul-searching that Arjun chanced upon a weathered book in a neglected corner of a bookstore. Its title, "The Dance of Synchronicities," resonated with him in a way he couldn't articulate. Little did he know this book would evolve into a guiding light on his journey of resilience.

The book's pages unfurled stories of individuals confronting life's trials with unwavering courage, discovering solace in the intricate dance of synchronicities. Arjun found himself captivated by the notion that beneath the chaos, there existed an intricate pattern—a pattern capable of guiding him toward purpose and healing.

Arjun's gaze drifted to the park's pond, where ripples formed as a duck glided gracefully across the water's surface. Much like the duck's serene glide, his journey had been a dance of its own—an art of embracing life's ebbs and flows with grace.

In the midst of his park strolls, Arjun had encountered a venerable figure named Guruji. Though their conversation had been brief, its impact was profound.

"Resilience," Guruji imparted, "is not merely about standing strong in the storm. It's about bending without breaking, akin to a reed in the wind."

Those words resonated with Arjun on a profound level, becoming a mantra that steered him through life's tempests. He learned that resilience wasn't a rigid shield; it was the flexibility to adapt, the willingness to learn, and the strength to transform.

As Arjun continued his walks in the park, he observed the shifting seasons—a metaphor for the cyclical nature of life. Just as spring unfurled its petals after winter, moments of hardship were succeeded by glimpses of hope. And in those moments, he discovered synchronicities—the universe's gentle reminders that he was traversing the right path.

One winter morning, seated on a bench and lost in contemplation, Arjun's attention was drawn to a little girl joyfully feeding breadcrumbs to the birds. Her laughter echoed through the air, carrying a sense of pure joy. Unable to resist, he smiled, reminded that even in the face of challenges, life offered moments of beauty that were worth cherishing.

Arjun's journey took him to unexpected places, including the doors of an orphanage. There, he encountered children who had weathered unimaginable hardships with a resilience that belied their age. Their laughter and optimism stood as a testament to the remarkable endurance and thriving spirit within every human.

During a visit to the orphanage, Arjun shared his story with the children, speaking of the dance of synchronicities and the transformative power of resilience. Their wide-eyed attention filled him with a profound sense of purpose, a realization that his journey wasn't solely for personal growth but to inspire others as well.

The journey also led Arjun to unforeseen friendships, such as the one he forged with Aisha—a woman whose life resembled a mosaic of challenges and triumphs. Their conversations were marked by a shared understanding of the dance of synchronicities. "Resilience," Aisha declared, "is the song we carry within us, a melody of strength that guides us through the darkest nights."

Amidst life's challenges, Arjun learned to uncover beauty in the details—a skill cultivated through mindfulness. Whether it was the hues of a sunset or the rhythm of rain against his window, he discovered that moments of presence wielded profound influence, serving as powerful tools of resilience.

Standing beside a blooming rosebush one day, Arjun was reminded of a profound quote he had encountered: "The rose's rarest essence lives in the thorns." These words resonated deeply, encapsulating the essence of his journey. He had discovered strength not in spite of challenges but because of them.

As the sun dipped below the horizon, casting long shadows across the park, Arjun's thoughts returned to the present. His journey of resilience stood as a testament to the dance of synchronicities—a dance that led him to unexpected places, introduced him to kindred spirits, and taught him the art of embracing life in all its shades.

Arjun's phone buzzed, interrupting his reverie. A message from Rahul appeared their friendship a constant reminder of the resilience nurtured in the soil of shared challenges. "Meet you at our spot tomorrow," the message read. Arjun's heart swelled with gratitude for friends who had become pillars of strength.

Leaving the park and walking towards the city's lights, Arjun's steps were lighter, his spirit unburdened. He had learned that resilience wasn't about avoiding life's storms but dancing with them—turning adversity into art and discovering synchronicities in the most unexpected corners of existence.

The journey had been his, but the lessons were universal—lessons of bending without breaking, of finding beauty in the midst of chaos, and of embracing the dance of synchronicities with an open heart. As Arjun navigated the city's bustling streets, he carried not only the wisdom gained from his own experiences but also the belief that, like the rose's rare essence residing in its thorns, strength often blossoms in the heart of life's challenges.

The Resonant Harmony

Embarking on the journey of embracing the harmonious crescendo, Arjun uncovered that the symphony of life held endless verses yet to be explored. The dance of synchronicities continued to weave its enchanting patterns, each thread revealing a new depth of meaning, a new layer of resonance.

In a quaint village secluded from the bustling world, Arjun found himself drawn to an ancient sage—a figure whose eyes held the wisdom of millennia. They sat by the side of a serene river, its gentle flow mirroring the rhythm of existence itself. The sage spoke of the unending cadence of life, the interconnectedness between all living things, and the symphony that reverberated across the cosmos.

As Arjun shared his own journey of resilience and synchronicities, the sage's eyes twinkled with understanding. "Life's symphony is a masterpiece," he mused, his voice carrying the weight of eternity. "And within this symphony, each soul has a unique melody to contribute."

Stirred by the sage's words, Arjun embarked on an inward quest—a journey to unearth the timeless truths dormant within him. He sought solace in meditation, in the rustling leaves of ancient forests, and in the whispered secrets of distant mountains.

During these moments of introspection, Arjun experienced an awakening—a profound realization that the dance of synchronicities was not a random sequence of events but a language through which the universe communicated its divine guidance. With this newfound understanding, Arjun felt an innate responsibility to share the wisdom of synchronicities with the world. He recognized that his journey was intertwined with the journey of every other soul, all seeking to harmonize their individual melodies with the grand cosmic composition.

Arjun's workshops and retreats blossomed into sanctuaries for souls yearning to rediscover their own symphonies within, from every corner of the world, seekers, artists, leaders, and dreamers congregated—united by the magnetic pull of synchronicities. These gatherings nurtured a community bound by the shared desire to dance in rhythm with the universe's cadence.

During one transformative retreat, Arjun crossed paths with Meera—a woman whose life had been etched with heartache and trials. Through the teachings of synchronicities, Meera began recognizing the hidden harmonies of resilience and hope that had guided her journey.

Beneath the starlit sky, surrounded by the warmth of a crackling bonfire, Meera bared her soul. Her voice, laced with raw emotion, echoed as she unveiled the story of her personal dance of synchronicities. "Even amidst the darkest notes," she whispered, her eyes gleaming with unwavering resolve, "there is a symphony of courage and strength."

Her words reverberated, becoming a chord that struck a harmonious note within each individual present. Arjun realized that his journey of resilience and synchronicities had evolved into a symphony of transformation, its echoes extending far beyond his own path.

As the years unfolded like verses of a cosmic poem, Arjun's influence expanded. His workshops transformed into havens of wisdom, drawing souls eager to unite their stories with the universal narrative. Through it all, Arjun sensed the guiding hand of the universe—the same hand that had led him to Rahul, Kavya, and Amrita.

He comprehended that the dance of synchronicities was an unending melody, guiding him to explore new horizons, encounter fresh experiences, and uncover deeper truths. Life's symphony was a composition forever evolving, and Arjun felt honored to play his part. In the grand orchestration of existence, he realized that every soul, including his own, contributed a unique and irreplaceable note to the eternal melody of life.

From the majestic peak, surveying the sprawling landscape below, Arjun felt a surge of gratitude washing over him. He acknowledged that his journey was a precious gift—an opportunity to uncover the symphony residing within his soul.

In the intricate tapestry of existence, Arjun had discovered his own unique melody—a tune resonating with resilience, love, and the interconnectedness of all life. It was a melody destined to echo for eons, a symphony of grace and beauty harmonizing with the hearts of all who swayed to the universe's rhythms.

With a heart brimming with reverence and adoration, Arjun continued to waltz with life's symphony. He surrendered to the universe's embrace, entrusting himself to its melodies and harmonies, both seen and unseen.

Embracing the harmonious crescendo of his odyssey, Arjun recognized that he was forever entwined in the cosmic dance—a living testament to the enduring enchantment of synchronicities and the boundless fortitude of the human spirit.

As the final notes of the symphony caressed the air, Arjun closed his eyes, attuned to the eternal rhythm pulsating through his very essence. The dance of synchronicities would forever be his guide, transcending the constraints of time and space.

With a heart overflowing with love, gratitude, and unyielding resilience, Arjun surrendered to the symphony of the universe. He understood that he was eternally interwoven in its melodies—a living embodiment of the everlasting magic of synchronicities and the indomitable strength of the human soul.

Arjun's embrace of the harmonious crescendo unfolded like an intricate symphony, each note a testament to the depth of his journey. The dance of synchronicities painted vibrant hues across the canvas of his life, revealing patterns of meaning and connection that resonated with his very soul.

In a remote hamlet veiled by nature's tranquillity, Arjun found himself drawn to an aged sage—a sage whose eyes held the wisdom of ages long past. They settled by a tranquil riverbank, its gentle murmurs a reflection of the timeless rhythm of existence. The sage spoke of life's eternal cadence, the thread of unity binding all living beings, and the symphony that echoed through the cosmos.

As Arjun shared his own tale of resilience and synchronicities, the sage's gaze sparkled with understanding. "Life's symphony is a masterpiece, my friend," he intoned, his voice a mellifluous echo of ages gone by. "And within this masterpiece, every individual carries a melody uniquely their own."

Arjun, stirred by the sage's words, embarked on an inner voyage—a pilgrimage to uncover the ageless truths dormant within his being. He found solace in the silence of meditation, in the whispering secrets of ancient woods, and in the embrace of towering mountains.

In these moments of introspection, a revelation dawned upon Arjun—a profound understanding that the dance of synchronicities was not a random sequence of events but a cosmic language of guidance and connection.

Amidst the silent rustle of leaves and the distant echoes of the river, Arjun unearthed the buried whispers of his soul. Each breath became a rhythmic dance with the universe, a sacred communion between his essence and the cosmic forces that shaped his destiny.

With the sage as his guide through this labyrinth of self-discovery, Arjun felt the weight of his past lift. The aged trees, witnesses to Arjun's revelations, stood tall like guardians of ancient secrets, their leaves whispering tales of endurance.

As the sun dipped below the horizon, casting a golden glow upon the landscape, Arjun realized that his journey was intertwined with the very fabric of existence. The river, a metaphor for the ever-flowing current of time, mirrored the constant flux of life's experiences.

"In the hushed whispers of the woods," mused Arjun, "I found the fragrant promise of new beginnings. Life's symphony, with its intricate notes, is a tapestry woven by every soul, each contributing a melody uniquely its own."

In the shadow of towering mountains, Arjun's awareness expanded. The panorama of his existence shifted, revealing a kaleidoscope of interconnected moments. Each revelation was a brushstroke on the canvas of his destiny, creating a masterpiece that echoed the universal truth of interconnectedness.

Empowered by this newfound insight, Arjun embraced a deep-seated duty to share the wisdom of synchronicities with the world. His own journey, now intertwined with the journeys of countless others, became a guiding light for those seeking to harmonize their melodies with the grand tapestry of existence.

"

Discover your unique talents, pursue your passions, and let your authenticity illuminate the path to an enchanting life

"

11

The Orchestration of Life

September 11, 2022

Ever changing Kaleidoscope

Arjun stood on the precipice of another momentous chapter in his life, an oasis of reflection amidst the bustling heartbeat of Mumbai. The journey that had brought him here unfolded as a symphony of serendipity and self-discovery, an intricate dance where resilience waltzed with wisdom.

The vibrant streets of Mumbai, illuminated by a tapestry of colorful lights, mirrored the kaleidoscope of emotions swirling within Arjun's heart. Gracefully weaving through the city's bustling crowds, his mind resonated with vivid memories—a symphony of experiences that painted the canvas of his life with vibrant hues.

These memories, like strokes of brilliance, transported him back to Varanasi's spiritual embrace, where the Ganges whispered ancient secrets, and time seemed suspended. The misty tea gardens of Darjeeling, where the morning mist enveloped him in an ethereal embrace, remained etched in his mind like a melodic refrain. Each place a note in the grand composition of his life.

As Arjun navigated the streets, the vibrancy around him echoed the vibrancy within him—a reflection of his transformative choices. Among these choices, the pivotal decision to forsake the comforts of corporate life and embrace a path of travel and storytelling stood as a testament to his courage and unyielding determination.

The solo journey that ensued, a traverse through the heart and soul of India, wove a tapestry with threads of uncertainty and curiosity. Despite skeptics questioning his choice, Arjun recognized this as his voyage of self-discovery, a daring leap into the unknown destined to sculpt the narrative of his life.

The essence of connection crystallized for Arjun beneath the starlit skies of Himachal Pradesh one night. Gathered around a bonfire amidst strangers who swiftly transformed into lifelong companions, he came to the profound realization that human bonds transcend physical boundaries. The symphony of camaraderie he experienced echoed a universal truth—hearts united by stories, effortlessly bridging the gaps of geography and culture.

As months unfolded like the notes of a melody, Arjun's journey carried him to mountain monasteries and sun-soaked beaches alike. He meditated with serene monks, allowing the mountains' whispers to guide him. On serene shores, he practiced yoga, synchronizing his breath with the rhythmic waves. Ancient scriptures beckoned, revealing timeless wisdom as he sought answers to the profound riddles of existence.

Within life's crescendos and lulls, Arjun mastered the art of resilience, learning to dance gracefully with uncertainty. He discerned that life's twists and turns were not adversaries but rather the very building blocks of his journey. Each obstacle etched a line on the canvas of his destiny, and he embraced them all with the fortitude of a seasoned traveler.

Amid Mumbai's vibrant rhythms, Arjun's heart resonated with a symphony of gratitude for every experience that had sculpted him. It wasn't the destinations that defined his journey but the tapestry of moments woven together. His path stood as a testament to the extraordinary within the ordinary, a celebration of life's everyday notes composing his unique melody.

A vivid memory surfaced—encountering nomads during a Himalayan trek, free spirits unburdened by the shackles of routine. Their way of life imprinted upon him a commitment to live each day with the same freedom and embrace the unknown with open arms.

Yet, Arjun's journey extended beyond the landscapes he traversed; it delved into the landscapes within. Meditation served as his compass, guiding him to the stillness within himself. Amidst life's clamor, he discovered his sanctuary—a space where his inner symphony harmonized with the universe's cosmic melody.

Arjun realized that harmony with the world around him was rooted in inner harmony. He dared to explore his emotions, confronting fears and vulnerabilities with unwavering resolve. Through the shadows, he unearthed a strength—the kind that emerges when one faces oneself without pretense.

As his inner symphony evolved, so did his interactions with others. Empathy blossomed, understanding deepened, and compassion flowed freely. He recognized that each individual carried their own melody, and rather than imposing his own notes, he extended a helping hand, a comforting presence.

Empowered by this newfound wisdom, Arjun discerned his calling—to pen down his captivating encounters and revelations, weaving his tales into a symphony of inspiration. His words became an anthem for embracing life's journey—capturing the rhythm of each heart, the cadence of every soul, and the beauty between the notes.

Arjun's narrative continued to echo, reminding everyone that extraordinary moments reside within the ordinary. Each day, each encounter, held the potential for magic, and it was within life's rhythm that courage, compassion, and love painted their masterpiece. His story was an invitation to dance with life's ever-changing kaleidoscope, to relish each color and every shift.

Dear reader, as you immerse yourself in Arjun's symphony, may you find the courage to dance to life's diverse tunes. May you embrace each note, each pause, and uncover your own kaleidoscope of experiences. For within you resides a melody—a unique tapestry woven with the threads of courage and self-discovery, waiting to unfurl its vibrant colors to the world.

The odyssey of Arjun continued to unfold—a mesmerizing narrative enticing readers to delve deeper into the symphony of his life. With each step he took, the orchestration of destiny played on, and the kaleidoscope of experiences spun its enchanting patterns.

Immersed in the vibrant rhythm of the city, Arjun discerned parallels between the bustling streets and the intricate tapestry of his own journey. The teeming crowds mirrored the myriad encounters that had shaped him—each a brushstroke on the canvas of his existence.

Mumbai's kaleidoscope of lights served as a fitting backdrop for his reflections. Just as the city dazzled with its diversity, Arjun's experiences across India had painted his life with myriad shades—rich, vivid, and unforgettable. The streets reverberated with echoes of his travels, and memories resurfaced like notes of a haunting melody.

From the spiritual haven of Varanasi to the tranquil tea gardens of Darjeeling, Arjun had wandered through landscapes that mirrored the diverse terrain of his own soul. These places weren't merely destinations; they were chapters that had sculpted him into a maestro of resilience and wisdom.

Amidst the luminous tapestry of Mumbai, Arjun's thoughts rewound to a pivotal moment—the day he shed the corporate façade to embrace his true calling. Amid skepticism and caution, he embarked on a solo journey across India—a journey that defied conventions and redefined his very essence.

Yet, it was beneath the starlit canopy of Himachal Pradesh that the essence of connection took root in Arjun's heart. As the flames of a bonfire flickered in rhythm with the whispers of the night, strangers morphed into kindred spirits. In that magical moment, he realized that humanity's symphony played a tune of unity, transcending barriers and differences.

The symphony of experiences continued to carry Arjun further—mountain monasteries and sun-kissed beaches whispered their secrets and ancient scriptures unveiled profound truths. Through meditation and introspection, Arjun discovered the echoes of eternity in his own soul. The tranquil mountains became his confidants, and the waves on pristine shores whispered age-old wisdom.

In the ebb and flow of his journey, Arjun mastered the art of resilience. The uncertainties that once seemed daunting transformed into stepping stones on his path. He recognized that each twist and turn was a brushstroke on the canvas of his life, contributing to a tapestry that was uniquely his.

Amid Mumbai's vivacious rhythm, Arjun's heart echoed with gratitude for every encounter that had shaped him. The experiences had woven a rich tapestry— each moment a stroke of brilliance, each challenge a touch of color. It was a tapestry that transformed his perspective, a vibrant reminder that life's true beauty resided in the ordinary.

A memory surged forth—a meeting with nomads on a Himalayan trail, their carefree existence a lesson in freedom and authenticity. The encounter engraved a commitment in Arjun's heart—to embrace life with open arms and savor each day as a gift.

Yet, the journey didn't end with geographical landscapes; it delved into the landscapes within. Meditation became his guide, leading him to the sanctuary of his own soul. Amidst life's cacophony, he discovered an inner symphony that resonated with the universe's eternal melody.

Arjun's realization dawned—a harmonious connection with the world required finding harmony within. He delved into the depths of his emotions, confronting fears and vulnerabilities with unyielding courage. The shadows within him transformed into stepping stones to self-discovery, a testament to his resilience.

With the evolution of his inner symphony, Arjun's interactions with others underwent a profound transformation. Empathy became his compass, and understanding his creed. Recognizing the universality of human struggles, he extended a helping hand—a reassuring presence to those he encountered.

Bolstered by this newfound insight, Arjun embraced his higher purpose—to translate his extraordinary experiences into words, weaving them into a tapestry of inspiration. Through his stories, he aimed to awaken others to life's symphony—a composition of hearts beating in unison, souls dancing to their own rhythm.

Arjun's tale continued to resonate—an ode to the extraordinary that resides within the ordinary. His narrative spoke of life's quiet miracles, urging all to perceive the magic in everyday moments. Each day, each step, was an opportunity to paint life's canvas with courage, compassion, and boundless love.

As his story unfolded, it resonated with readers, urging them to embark on their own journeys of discovery. The symphony of Arjun's life became a symphony of countless souls—each embracing their unique path, harmonizing with the world's melody.

Dear reader, as you journey through Arjun's symphony, may you find the courage to embrace life's kaleidoscope. May you dance to your own rhythm, savor every note, and cherish every pause. Within you lies an exquisite tapestry of experiences waiting to be unveiled— an invitation to let life's melody resonate through your very being.

The Melodies of Connection

Arjun's journey persisted—an uncharted voyage through the tapestry of existence that unfolded like a grand symphony before him. The world's vivid landscapes and the souls that inhabited them left indelible marks upon his heart. In this odyssey, he learned that life was not a solitary composition but a harmonious collaboration of faces, places, and moments, each contributing a unique note to the symphony of existence.

The captivating city of Udaipur often hailed as the Venice of the East, beckoned Arjun with its enchanting allure. Amidst its serene lakes and regal palaces, he encountered Kavita, a gifted artist whose canvases seemed to hold fragments of her very soul. Her art was a reflection of life's myriad hues—its vibrant colors, deep emotions, and the intricate dance of light and shadow.

Arjun listened raptly as Kavita bared her journey—a tale interwoven with trials, a vulnerable artist's path, and the triumph of unwavering passion. Her life was a symphony in its own right, with crescendos of success and the contemplative pauses of an artist deep in thought. In her company, Arjun found a kindred spirit, someone who understood the alchemy of aligning one's soul with the world's diverse symphony.

As the hours slipped away, Kavita shared her profound conviction that art possessed the power to mend and forge connections between souls. Her words resonated within Arjun, echoing the truth that amidst life's cacophony, art had the uncanny ability to create bridges that spanned differences and united hearts in resonance.

Kavita's perspective struck a chord within him, igniting the realization that life's symphony wasn't confined to concert halls or galleries. Every action, every intention, every connection—they all composed the rich tapestry of life's symphony, woven with threads of emotions and experiences.

Contemplating the transformative encounters of his journey, Arjun reminisced about the children of Kolkata—little maestros crafting melodies of joy with makeshift instruments in narrow alleys. Their laughter echoed through the air, serving as a poignant reminder that life's most exquisite harmonies often emerged in spontaneous, unscripted moments.

Seated amidst the children, Arjun clapped and swayed, carried away by their rhythm. In that shared moment, he sensed the universal language of the symphony—a language transcending age, nationality, and background, fostering connections that were authentic and profound.

Arjun's odyssey uncovered unexpected connections in diverse places. Amid the arid landscapes of Rajasthan, he encountered a group of women harmoniously singing folk songs while toiling in the fields. Their melodies carried the weight of life stories—joys, sorrows, struggles, and victories. As he listened, Arjun felt an inexplicable bond with the land and its people—a reminder that the symphony of existence echoed the rhythms of nature and the collective human experience.

Delhi introduced Arjun to Rahul, an impassioned social entrepreneur dedicated to empowering underprivileged youth through education and skill development. Conversations with Rahul revealed that the symphony of life wasn't merely an individual pursuit; it was a symphony where every selfless act, regardless of scale, could resonate into waves of transformation, shaping the very fabric of society.

Arjun's odyssey unfolded as an uncharted exploration through the rich tapestry of existence, akin to a grand symphony that gradually revealed its complexity with each step. The landscapes he traversed and the souls he encountered left profound imprints on his consciousness. Life, he discerned, was not a solitary melody but a harmonious collaboration of diverse faces, places, and moments, each contributing a unique note to the intricate orchestration of existence.

Udaipur, a city often likened to the Venice of the East, extended a captivating invitation to Arjun. Amidst the tranquil lakes and regal palaces, he found himself drawn to Kavita, a gifted artist whose canvases seemed to hold fragments of her very essence. Her art was not merely a visual representation but an embodiment of life's nuanced hues—vibrant colors, deep emotions, and the delicate interplay of light and shadow.

In Kavita's presence, Arjun discovered a kindred spirit, someone who comprehended the profound alchemy of aligning one's soul with the diverse symphony of the world. As the hours unfurled in their conversation, Kavita shared her conviction in the transformative power of art. It was not merely a medium of expression but a force capable of mending and forging connections between souls, transcending the boundaries of language and culture.

Contemplating the transformative encounters of his journey, Arjun reminisced about the vibrant alleys of Kolkata. There, he witnessed a group of children joyfully crafting melodies on improvised instruments. Their laughter echoed, creating harmonies that resonated with pure, unadulterated joy. In that unscripted moment, Arjun realized that life's most beautiful compositions were often spontaneous, emerging without the constraints of structure or expectation.

Immersing himself in their world, Arjun clapped and swayed to their rhythm. The language of the symphony spoke through their spontaneous connection—a language that transcended age, nationality, and background, revealing the universal thread that bound humanity together.

Arjun's expedition spanned diverse narratives—encounters with artists, educators, activists, and entrepreneurs—all contributing their unique notes to the grand composition of humanity. In the tranquil backwaters of Kerala, he connected with fishermen whose lives ebbed and flowed with the rhythm of the tides. Their tales unfolded as a testament to the symphony's ability to find solace in simplicity amidst the challenges of their daily struggles.

Varanasi, steeped in centuries of tradition, unveiled rituals along the Ganges, where prayers seamlessly merged with the river's gentle currents. Arjun realized that life's symphony wasn't confined to a single moment; it was a timeless composition sung by generations past and present. Each life, he understood, was a melody that intertwined with others, harmonizing to create a rich mosaic of existence.

Ultimately, Arjun comprehended that life's symphony wasn't a predetermined path but an ongoing dance of connections woven together to form a vibrant tapestry of experiences, relationships, and emotions—a symphony that embraced both harmonious and dissonant notes.

As he stood by the Ganges, the sun dipping below the horizon, Arjun felt a profound gratitude for his journey. The symphony of life unveiled the power of human connection, the beauty of embracing uncertainty, and the strength of resilience in the face of adversity.

With each passing day, Arjun's reverence for life's symphony deepened. He recognized that the journey was far from over, and he welcomed the new melodies that awaited him.

Dear reader, as you embark on your own symphony of life, may you embrace the connections that intertwine its notes. Dance to the melody of the unknown, savor the uniqueness of every chord and discover harmony within the diverse experiences that define your existence.

For within the grand symphony of life, your part is indispensable, and every moment presents an opportunity to contribute to the timeless melody that will resound for eternity.

The Crescendo of Fulfilment

Arjun's transformative odyssey unfolded amidst the serene valleys of Himachal Pradesh, where majestic mountains embraced verdant landscapes, creating a breathtaking backdrop for his journey. The air seemed to carry whispers of ancient wisdom, harmonizing with the melodies of nature that synchronized with the rhythm of his heart.

In this idyllic haven, Arjun's path intersected with Guruji, a sage whose eyes shimmered with the profundity of timeless knowledge. Guruji's tranquil smile and the aura of inner tranquility that surrounded him resonated deep within Arjun's soul.

Days seamlessly transformed into profound conversations as Arjun delved into discussions that spanned the spectrum of existence—love, purpose, and fulfillment. Guruji's teachings bore a resonance beyond the ordinary as if woven into the very fabric of the universe itself.

Guruji dispelled the notion that every individual was merely a vessel; rather, he illuminated the potential for greatness within each as a repository of divine consciousness. Each pearl of wisdom slipping from Guruji's lips felt like a puzzle piece clicking into place, revealing a profound sense of completion for Arjun.

Guruji's words unveiled life's symphony as a celestial masterpiece—an intricate tapestry meticulously woven by the universe. Arjun's vision cleared as he absorbed the profundity—his purpose was revealed, his path illuminated.

Guided by Guruji, Arjun learned the art of embracing the present moment—a skill resonating harmoniously with the symphony of life. Realization, Guruji imparted, thrived in the alignment with one's essence and the harmonization of one's purpose, independent of external gains.

Under Guruji's benevolent gaze, Arjun unlocked the power of inner peace—a force emanating from within, influencing every interaction. Life's symphony, he realized, wasn't solely about personal growth; it was a collective harmony where every individual's notes intertwined.

With newfound wisdom and overwhelming gratitude, Arjun bid adieu to Guruji, understanding that their meeting was a serendipitous thread woven into the tapestry of his journey.

The journey progressed to the vibrant city of Mumbai—a metropolis pulsating with energy and aspiration. Here, Arjun crossed paths with Maya—an embodiment of dynamism and success. Maya's journey struck a chord within Arjun, for her path had been a labyrinth of challenges navigated with tenacity.

Maya's story unfolded as a symphony of resilience—a medley of setbacks and triumphant crescendos. She had stared adversity in the face, carving her path with unwavering belief in her dreams. Through her tale, Arjun realized that the symphony of life wasn't always a harmonious melody; it was a composition resonating with dissonance and triumph.

Maya's success became a symphony of achievements, revealing that purpose transcended material possessions. It wasn't merely the destination that held meaning; the symphony was found in every step taken toward it.

Through Maya's narrative, Arjun's understanding of the symphony deepened. The symphony, he comprehended, wasn't a linear progression; it encompassed both highs and lows.

The final chapter of Arjun's odyssey unfolded amidst the tranquil backdrop of the Himalayan foothills, home to a monastery where devoted monks resided. Here, Arjun immersed himself in mindfulness—a practice that taught him the symphony of the present moment. The symphony of life, he learned, resonated in the eternal present, unconstrained by the past or future.

The monks imparted the art of introspection, revealing that the symphony was an internal journey as much as an external one. In their presence, Arjun glimpsed the symphony's ethereal layers—an exploration of the self and a dance of interconnectedness with all existence.

As Arjun's transformative voyage drew to a close, he reflected on the experiences that had sculpted his soul and refined his understanding. The symphony had unfolded his soul's depth and the universe's vastness.

He comprehended his role in the cosmic symphony—an individual note in the grand composition. Each interaction, he understood, was an opportunity to contribute—infusing every note with love, authenticity, and compassion.

Standing at the threshold of a new beginning, Arjun felt a profound gratitude. The symphony of life, vast and enigmatic, had embraced him—a humbling part of its eternal dance.

Dear reader, as you turn the final pages of this narrative, may you carry with you the echoes of your own symphony. Embrace it with an open heart and a spirit of curiosity, for each note, each moment is a treasure—an invitation to compose a melody that reverberates through eternity.

In the closing act of Arjun's extraordinary expedition, the serene valleys of Himachal Pradesh set the stage—an ode to nature's splendor where mountains reached for the sky and greenery sprawled like an artist's canvas. Amidst this harmonious backdrop, Arjun's path led him to an encounter that would forever transform the cadence of his journey.

Guruji, a venerable sage, welcomed Arjun into his abode—a haven tucked away amidst the hills. Guruji's eyes held the twinkle of countless tales, and his presence exuded a serene wisdom that drew Arjun in like a moth to the flame.

In the cocoon of Guruji's teachings, Arjun found solace as they delved into life's most profound inquiries—love, purpose, and the symphony of fulfillment. Every word from Guruji's lips felt like an unraveling of mysteries, each phrase resonating with a deep-seated truth that hummed within Arjun's soul.

Within the confines of these exchanges, Guruji bestowed upon Arjun the revelation that each soul was a divine vessel, carrying the universe's wisdom within. As Arjun absorbed these words, it was as if the missing notes of his symphony had been unveiled, allowing him to grasp the grandeur of his purpose.

Guruji's wisdom painted life's symphony as a celestial masterpiece—a composition authored by the cosmos itself. Arjun felt the threads of his destiny align as Guruji's words guided him, unveiling his path with unparalleled clarity and purpose.

Immersed in Guruji's tutelage, Arjun uncovered the art of cherishing the present—an art that resonated harmoniously with the symphony of life. Guruji's teachings echoed in his heart, encouraging Arjun to find fulfillment not in external conquests but in resonating with one's own essence and the universe's rhythm.

As Arjun bid farewell to Guruji, he knew that their meeting was no accident; it was a profound note within the symphony of his journey—a melody that had been composed by the universe itself.

Continuing his sojourn, Arjun ventured into the heart of Mumbai— an urban tapestry woven with dreams and ambition. Amidst this bustling backdrop, Arjun's path intersected with Maya—an embodiment of resilience and achievement. Maya's narrative struck a chord deep within Arjun, for her journey was a testament to the symphony of persistence.

Maya's story was a symphony of triumph over trials—a symphony composed of crescendos of triumph after every setback. Her journey was not just a linear progression of success; it was a testament to the symphony's ability to harmonize the dissonance of life's challenges.

Through Maya's story, Arjun learned that life's symphony wasn't a serene melody; it was a cacophony of struggles and triumphs, challenges and victories. Yet, within this chaos, there was beauty— beauty found in the pursuit of purpose and in the tapestry woven by each note of experience.

Maya's tale illuminated the symphony's essence—a tapestry of growth, both personal and collective. The symphony, Arjun realized, wasn't just about reaching a destination; it was about cherishing every step of the journey and finding fulfillment in the pursuit itself.

Arjun's comprehension of the symphony deepened as he embarked on the final chapter of his odyssey—a chapter set against the tranquil backdrop of the Himalayan foothills, home to a monastery where devoted monks resided.

Here, Arjun immersed himself in mindfulness—a practice that taught him the symphony of the present moment. Through meditation and the monks' guidance, he recognized that life's symphony wasn't confined to the past or the future; it was an eternal composition resonating in the present.

The monks imparted the art of introspection, revealing that the symphony was as much an internal journey as an external one. In their presence, Arjun glimpsed the symphony's ethereal layers—an exploration of the self and a dance of interconnectedness with all existence.

As Arjun's transformative voyage drew to a close, he looked back at the experiences that had sculpted his soul and refined his understanding. The symphony had led him through a labyrinth of revelations, showing him the symphony's intricate threads, its crescendos of triumphs and dissonances of challenges.

Arjun perceived himself as an instrument in the universe's symphony—a note played with love, compassion, and authenticity. Each interaction, he realized, was a chance to contribute to the grand symphony—a harmony of souls resonating through time.

Standing at the threshold of a new beginning, Arjun felt a profound gratitude. The symphony of life had enveloped him—a participant in its eternal dance, a note in its grand composition.

As you conclude this chapter, dear reader, carry with you the echoes of your own symphony. Embrace it with an open heart and a thirst for adventure, for every note, every moment, is an invitation to create a melody that shall echo through eternity.

“

Valuing relationships,
extending helping hands, and
collaborating together celebrate
the interconnectedness of life

”

The Masterpiece Unveiled

December 2, 2022 to April 1, 2024

Amidst the enveloping twilight, a café in Mumbai transformed into a sanctuary for introspection. Arjun and Aaradhya, two souls meandering through the crossroads of reflection and gratitude, cradled chai cups in their hands. Their hearts resonated with the symphony of a journey that transcended the confines of time and space, a voyage weaving resilience into a mesmerizing tapestry spanning two years. As the final chords of this odyssey unfurled, emotions converged into a mosaic—gratitude, fulfillment, and the bittersweet taste of parting.

The sun surrendered its reign to the horizon, casting hues of gold and amber across the sky while the city's pulse reverberated beneath a tranquil façade. Aaradhya's gaze served as a window into the depths of her thoughts, a distant contemplation etched across her features. "Two years since we embarked on this transformative journey," she mused softly, her words carrying the weight of an odyssey both tangible and metaphysical. "Yet, it feels as if it were only yesterday."

Arjun's eyes met hers, a knowing smile curving his lips. "Time becomes an illusion when the journey is intricately woven into the fabric of our souls."

Their odyssey had navigated the heart of India, traversing landscapes of resilience held close by the nation. From the towering Himalayan peaks whispering ancient tales to the sun-drenched beaches of Goa, where the laughter of the resilient mingled with the ocean's sighs—each step became a note in the grand symphony of resilience. It was a journey not confined to geographical terrains but one that unfolded through the corridors of their very beings.

The café, a sanctum where recollections flowed like a gentle river, witnessed tales of the ordinary unfolding into the extraordinary. This journey, initially about unveiling stories of resilience in others, had unveiled the hidden strength within themselves. Arjun's fingers traced intricate patterns on the cup's rim as he voiced his thoughts. "In our pursuit to capture narratives of resilience in others, we discovered our own symphony of endurance."

Aaradhya's gaze swirled with the dance of remembrance. "Indeed, and as we composed our own chapters of resilience, we discovered that life's rhythm isn't just in the highs—it's in embracing our vulnerabilities and harmonizing with the ebbs and flows."

The journey hadn't unfolded without its crescendos of difficulty. In the realm of dreams, there were moments of dissonance, doubts that cast shadows, and the apprehension of uncharted territories. Yet, it was precisely in these moments of testing that their true potential had risen to the forefront. The symphony, after all, wasn't about smooth transitions—it was about navigating through complex harmonies and forging a melody that resonated with souls.

As the evening's veil enveloped them, their conversation meandered around the individuals who had etched their stories on their hearts. They spoke of the resilient street vendor in Delhi, the unyielding fisherman in Kerala, and the myriad others who had lent their tales to this mosaic.

"The journey," Arjun mused, his voice a gentle melody, "taught us a profound truth—that resilience isn't an emblem of invincibility but a dance with our vulnerabilities."

Aaradhya nodded, her eyes reflecting a wellspring of understanding. "Our lyrics echo that sentiment—' Every scar, a story of grace, an ode to humanity's remarkable embrace.'"

The grand finale had unfolded as a concert, a symphony of resilience set to music, a tribute to human strength, and the conviction that the ordinary could transcend into the extraordinary. It wasn't merely a performance; it was an offering, a note of gratitude to every inspiration, a homage to the indomitable spirit, and a reminder that within each life resides the potential for the extraordinary.

As the night unfurled, they left the café, their steps guiding them along the crescent of Marine Drive. The city's lights were a celestial tapestry, and the sea's breeze whispered ancient secrets. Amidst this urban dynamism, they discovered a haven of stillness—a moment to reflect upon the masterpiece that had been their journey.

"Remember when we embarked on this odyssey?" Aaradhya's voice was a whisper, a brushstroke on the canvas of the night.

Arjun's smile remained the memory etched vividly in his mind. "How could I forget? It was a leap into the unknown, an adventure where fear and excitement danced hand in hand."

"And look at us now," Aaradhya remarked, her eyes sparkling with pride. "We've journeyed, we've evolved, and we've dared to dream."

Arjun's hand found hers, a symbol of unity and shared purpose. "Indeed, we have. But this is just the prelude. The symphony of our lives is far from its final crescendo."

Their expedition had completed its orbit. What had initially been an exploration of resilience had blossomed into an intimate revelation. They had discovered the essence of resilience within themselves—the rhythm, the power, and the unwavering grace. Standing by the sea, bathed in the lustrous embrace of the night sky, they comprehended that their masterpiece was but in its opening bars.

The chapters that ensued witnessed Arjun and Aaradhya composing music that whispered of humanity's enduring spirit. Their melodies weren't mere notes; they were a clarion call of hope and courage that resonated far beyond geographical confines. They traversed continents, unearthing the tapestry of resilience woven into diverse cultures, seamlessly weaving their experiences into their harmonies.

Their music wasn't confined to the heart; it echoed in the corridors of change. Through their altruistic endeavors, they illuminated the path for the less fortunate, becoming catalysts for education and empowerment.

In the cities they journeyed to, they embraced new narratives of resilience, each encounter deepening their faith in the human spirit. With every connection, the symphony's resonance expanded, amplifying the heartbeat of the resilient.

Underneath the stars, enveloped in the serene aftermath of yet another triumphant performance, Aaradhya turned to Arjun with a question laden with memories. "Remember when we deliberated over the title for our journey's chronicle? And we chose 'Symphony of Resilience'?"

Arjun's eyes crinkled with the weight of shared memories. "How could I forget? It feels like a lifetime ago."

"Doesn't it seem the perfect epitome now?" Aaradhya's voice held the essence of contemplation. "Our journey—life itself—is a symphony. It's the interplay of crescendos and decrescendos, of moments that stretch and soar. And at its core, the symphony's soul is the indomitable spirit of resilience."

Arjun's smile mirrored her sentiment. "You're absolutely right. Life is a symphony, and every one of us, a musician, contributing a unique note to the grand tapestry of humanity."

Their expedition had laid bare a profound truth—resilience wasn't an elusive art confined to the extraordinary. It was an intrinsic quality harbored by every soul, a dormant ember awaiting the spark of discovery, nurture, and celebration.

As they navigated the uncharted melodies of existence, Arjun and Aaradhya understood that their masterpiece wasn't a static creation. It was a symphony in motion—a journey, an exploration, and a celebration of the resilience woven into the very fabric of life.

The Arabian Sea whispered its secrets to the night, and the city's heartbeat resonated in the distance. Arjun and Aaradhya stood at the cusp of destiny, gazing at the vast expanse of possibilities. Their hearts pulsated with gratitude, for the journey they had undertaken had led them to this very moment—the culmination of their masterpiece.

Their symphony had not reached its final note. Instead, it had become a never-ending opus, a testament to the boundless resilience that dwelled within them and within every being that graced this journey called life.

Facing the vast expanse of the sea, Arjun and Aaradhya recognized that their masterpiece was more than just a composition—it was a legacy of unyielding spirit, a tribute to the symphony of existence. The horizon painted itself in hues of wonder, mirroring the tapestry of their own lives.

"Life," Arjun spoke softly, "is a canvas of resilience where each experience becomes a stroke of courage, each challenge a stroke of determination."

Aaradhya's eyes sparkled, reflecting the shimmering sea. "And with each note we play, with each moment we embrace, we add to the symphony that resonates through time."

Their story continued a harmonious collaboration with life itself. Arjun and Aaradhya composed melodies of change, their music was painting the world with hues of hope. Their journey, a vivid testament to the symphony of resilience, echoed the truth that ordinary souls could weave extraordinary tales.

As they embarked on the uncharted melodies yet to be composed, their hearts were brimming with possibility. Their masterpiece, their symphony of resilience, had just begun its eternal dance, and they were ready to embrace every note, every crescendo, and every silence in between.

For in the grand orchestration of life, each note, each chord, and each movement was a gift—an opportunity to craft a melody that would linger in the hearts of generations, a legacy of resilience that would resonate through the ages.

And so, as the stars watched over their journey, Arjun and Aaradhya stepped into the embrace of the unknown, their souls harmonizing with the rhythm of existence. Their symphony of resilience was a timeless ode, a masterpiece that would forever remind the world of the incredible power that resided within the human spirit.

As they walked into the night, side by side, the echoes of their music lingered, a reminder that in the symphony of life, every note was a testament, every experience a melody, and every heart a musician. And as their footsteps faded into the night, the symphony of resilience continued a masterpiece that would never fade away.

A Melody of Eternity

In the vibrant tapestry of Mumbai's unyielding streets, Arjun and Aaradhya found themselves once again atop a skyscraper, the city sprawled below them like a pulsating heartbeat. This vantage point not only revealed the metropolis's grandeur but also served as a reminder of the infinite possibilities that danced in the nocturnal embrace.

Their journey, a profound odyssey through the kaleidoscope of human experience, had reached its zenith. Joyful symphonies and haunting descants had interwoven, creating a tapestry that adorned the recesses of their very souls. The resilience they had summoned echoed not just in their lives but resonated with kindred spirits who had trodden a parallel path, if only in the ethereal realm.

The city lights, a dazzling palette against the night's canvas, mirrored the threads of their collective experiences. Arjun, once tethered by societal norms, had metamorphosed into a man who embraced life's kaleidoscopic hues with an unguarded heart. Each chapter, from humble beginnings to extraordinary revelations, contributed to a mosaic that defied neat categorization.

Strengths that lay dormant had blossomed, fueled by the undulating waves of resilience he had conjured from the depths of his being. Aaradhya, his muse and confidante, had woven her melodies into the very fabric of his existence, creating a harmonious cadence that reverberated through the years.

What had started as a faint whisper of resilience had now crescendoed into the anthem of their lives? Its verses harmonized with the melodies of countless hearts, a testament to the enduring capacity of the human spirit to surmount challenges and ascend beyond adversity. The cityscape below, adorned with twinkling lights, bore witness to their transformative journey.

The impact of their symphony of resilience extended far beyond the confines of their personal narrative. Letters and messages arrived from distant corners, each a testament to the symphony's profound effect. Its notes of hope and courage resonated with individuals, inspiring them to seize the pen and rewrite the narratives of their own destinies. The rooftop, once a mere physical space, had transformed into a metaphorical stage where the anthem of resilience played on, inviting others to join the chorus and discover the unwritten chapters of their lives.

In the three years since their paths had converged, Arjun and Aaradhya had transcended the boundaries of individual experience. Their union had given rise to a symphony, a melodic narrative that unfolded against the vast canvas of life. Love, the cornerstone of their bond, emerged as a wellspring of strength and inspiration, resilient in the face of storms and exultant in moments of pure joy.

Their journey had illuminated the enchantment of serendipity and the beckoning call of the unknown. The crossroads they navigated underscored the notion that life's most transformative moments often lurk just beyond the comfort of the familiar. Embracing uncertainty became a key, unlocking a portal to a realm where possibilities stretched to the infinite, each choice casting ripples across the fabric of their existence.

Amidst the cadence of strength and the echoes of euphoria, Arjun discovered the potency of embracing vulnerability. His evolution bore witness to the profound beauty of resilience, where challenges were not impediments but gateways to personal growth. The symphony of life, he realized, was a composition of contradictions—a harmonious blend of laughter and tears, struggles and triumphs.

Aaradhya, his companion in this extraordinary journey, stood as both muse and collaborator in the crafting of their shared symphony. Her music, intertwined with the narrative, resonated as an echo of her soul's odyssey. Through her eyes, the world revealed itself anew, and within the cadence of her melodies, Arjun found solace in the harmonies of life.

Under the shimmering stars, Arjun and Aaradhya sensed the heartbeat of the city beneath them—a city that had been both spectator and participant in their metamorphosis. With each pulsation, they realized that their journey was not a destination but an ever-unfolding continuum. The symphony of resilience they had composed was not a concluding note but a melody that reverberated through the corridors of eternity.

As they gazed forward, acutely aware that life's grand composition would persist in its evolution, shaped by the relentless ebb and flow of time, Arjun and Aaradhya found solace in the constancy of their shared purpose—to inspire, uplift, and celebrate the indomitable human spirit. Armed with the lessons gleaned, the melodies meticulously composed, and the symphony deftly conducted, they stood poised to inscribe new chapters, each one a blank canvas awaiting the vibrant strokes of experience.

Hand in hand on the rooftop, where their journey had unfurled its inaugural notes, Arjun and Aaradhya embraced a profound sense of gratitude. Their love story, intricately woven into the symphony of resilience, had not only metamorphosed their own lives but had become a legacy destined to resonate through generations.

The symphony, conceived amid the bustling tapestry of Mumbai, had transcended geographical confines, resonating with the universal cadence of the human experience. It had whispered to dreamers, stoked the fires of determination, and ignited sparks of courage, reminding all that each life was a melody waiting to be sung and every journey a symphony yearning to be played.

In the gentle embrace of a breeze imbued with the scent of the sea, Arjun and Aaradhya acknowledged that their love story, though uniquely theirs, mirrored the myriad tales unfolding in every corner of the world. With this realization, they stepped into the night, prepared to compose fresh melodies, confront novel challenges, and perpetuate their journey of resilience.

In the symphony of life, devoid of final notes or ultimate destinations, they understood its perpetual state of evolution. Every moment, is a note contributing to a harmonious masterpiece, resonating through eternity. As Arjun and Aaradhya ventured into the night, the city whispered its secrets, the stars stood sentinel, and the symphony of resilience perpetuated its eternal melody.

Dear Readers

As I reach the culmination of the profound odyssey that is "Destiny's Kaleidoscope," my heart brims with profound gratitude and a sense of deep fulfillment. This literary labor of love has been a testament to resilience, and I extend my heartfelt appreciation to those whose unwavering support and inspiration have been the pillars of this endeavor.

Foremost among these pillars is my dear mother—my guiding light and wellspring of strength. Her boundless love and unyielding belief in my capabilities have propelled me through the intricate tapestry of writing this book. Her resilience in the face of challenges stands as a testament to the indomitable power of the human spirit.

Gratitude extends to the beautiful souls who have graced my journey. Be it friends, mentors, or strangers, each has left an indelible mark, contributing to the stories and insights etched onto these pages. Your courage, wisdom, and fortitude have been wellsprings of inspiration.

Life's lessons, both bitter and sweet, deserve a nod of appreciation. The trials and triumphs, the crests and troughs—all have been invaluable tutors. They've sculpted my understanding of resilience and the art of embracing life's uncertainties with grace and courage.

A debt of gratitude extends to the divine presence that has guided my path. To the universe to God, I offer thanks for the bestowed opportunities and blessings. Your guidance has fortified my spirit, encouraging me to delve into new horizons and unravel the depths of human resilience.

As "Destiny's Kaleidoscope" concludes, my heart resonates with gratitude, and I hope the echoes of this journey inspire others to explore the profound depths within themselves.

Lastly, to you, cherished readers, my gratitude knows no bounds. Thank you for joining me on this transformative 00odyssey for sharing your precious time and attention. It is my sincere hope that "Destiny's Kaleidoscope" has woven its threads into the tapestry of your heart and soul, sparking a resonance that encourages you to embrace your own resilience and rewrite the narratives of your life.

As we collectively turn the final page of this literary journey, let the wisdom linger—that life, much like a kaleidoscope, unfolds in a mosaic of moments, each ripe with the potential for growth, transformation, and resilience. Embrace the vibrant hues of your unique journey, and may you discover strength in the face of adversity, joy amidst challenges, and love in every nuance life brings your way.

With profound love and gratitude.

– Vikas Parihar